INVISIBLETHREADS

Also available in Definitions:

The Burning City by Ariel and Joaquín Dorfman

Corbenic by Catherine Fisher

Desire Lines by Jack Gantos

Malarkey by Keith Gray

Something in the Air by Jan Mark

The Shell House by Linda Newbery

Small Gains by K. M. Peyton

INVISIBLETHREADS

Annie Dalton & Maria Dalton

DEFINITIONS

INVISIBLE THREADS
A RED FOX BOOK 0 099 43338 9

First published in Great Britain by Red Fox,
an imprint of Random House Children's Books

This edition published 2004

1 3 5 7 9 10 8 6 4 2

Papers used by Random House Children's Books are natural, recyclable products made
from wood grown in sustainable forests. The manufacturing processes conform to the
environmental regulations of the country of origin.

Set in BauerBodoni and Gillsans

Red Fox Books are published by Random House Children's Books,
61–63 Uxbridge Road, London W5 5SA,
a division of The Random House Group Ltd,
in Australia by Random House Australia (Pty) Ltd,
20 Alfred Street, Milsons Point, Sydney, NSW 2061, Australia,
in New Zealand by Random House New Zealand Ltd,
18 Poland Road, Glenfield, Auckland 10, New Zealand,
and in South Africa by Random House (Pty) Ltd,
Endulini, 5A Jubilee Road, Parktown 2193, South Africa

THE RANDOM HOUSE GROUP Limited Reg. No. 954009
www.kidsatrandomhouse.co.uk

A CIP catalogue record for this book is available from the British Library.

Printed and bound in Great Britain by
Bookmarque Ltd, Croydon, Surrey

For Anna, Reuben and Maria, who lit up my life
the first moment I saw them; and still do! – AD

For Anna, Philipp and Reuben, with many thanks
and much love for all your support – MD

Carrie-Anne

Today I am sixteen years old. Today I have surpassed her.

Mum is all balloons and cream cakes.

'Come on, Carrie-Anne, love, smile!'

Click, flash, click, flash!

I am still not strong enough to claim my teenage right and roll my eyes, so I oblige, all eyes and teeth; I give her my best celebrity sparkle. With my mouth open and my teeth sharp I could devour her in one bite.

'Doesn't she look lovely?' My mum sighs, nudging my dad with a spiky elbow in his hard rib.

My dad grunts, a hog man hidden behind a broadsheet. He rustles his paper and gives me a pirate wink.

My dad understands me, because he knows my mum. We're comrades. I perform a perfect sashay towards the kitchen. I know my mum is watching my hips move softly side to side. She's envious of my ease and youth.

It's my birthday and I don't have to be nice.

Sarah's soaking corn flakes in a hand-painted Italian bowl. We've never been to Italy, but Mum thinks she can fool the neighbours into thinking our annual family nightmare in Devon is actually an art history tour of Tuscany. I curl my lip.

I'm sixteen today and I can think whatever I want.

Robert shuffles in, followed by a pristinely scrubbed Emma, my Jelly Bean. I am suddenly surrounded by three baby blonds. Sarah has soft curls framing a flower-fairy face. Her twin brother Robert's hair is short and spiky but fluffy like a duckling. Emma has Mum's hair. Fine strands of silk spilling down her back. A fairy-tale princess. She is sunshine.

I look at my golden brother and sisters and feel my darkness eclipse them. I am pitch-black, brow and hair. The happy golden siblings are joined by their happy golden parents. Karen and Derek Harris.

Click, flash, click, flash!

'Come on, kids, put your arms around Carrie-Anne. Go on, Emma, give her a big birthday kiss.'

If they're her kids, what am I? Her special baby? Her chosen child? I believed that until I was seven and friends began to pick and tease. I quickly realized that the translation and the truth behind my mother's words was: abandoned child, the trash baby who was thrown out with the rest of the crap.

This day, my birthday, reminds me that there is a woman out there, and by bone and by blood I belong to her. I am that woman's shame and regret.

Now I am sixteen and I have surpassed her. I've made it, I haven't messed up. I am clean and safe. I made it. The family history of Carrie-Anne and her mystery mum has a new chapter.

Click, flash, click, flash!

Naomi

I can hold you any time I like.

'You can hold that little baby any time you like.'
That's what the nurse tells me. She's not one of the hard-
cop, soft-cop midwives I had before, just this Irish nurse
with a tired face. She says it because she sees I'm upset.

Nine months, close as my own breath, now suddenly
you're public property. I can't see you, just their backs in
hospital gowns. They're sucking out your lungs with a
tube as if you're a piece of plumbing.

'We'll take you onto the ward in a minute, then you can
hold her any time you like. You'll be sick of her by the time
you get her home,' says the nurse in a soothing voice.

They're still concentrating on you, like mechanics
round an engine. The brutal sucking sounds make me
want to snatch you back, but they have to do it. It's so
you can breathe.

Oh God, oh God, suppose you couldn't breathe? And inside I'm praying, Be OK, baby. Please please be OK.

And you are, you are OK, because they lift me onto this trolley and cover me with a thin white blanket, and I get to hold you again. You're in a little nightie now and not so bloody, but your fuzzy hair is still black, deep jet-black like a blackbird's feathers.

It's the first time we've met yet suddenly we're rattling along corridors together, down ramps, in and out of lifts.

It feels dangerous, it feels out of control. Ceilings and light fittings fly over my head. Alarming sights jump out. Someone vomiting into a dish. Closed curtains with moaning going on behind. Over one woman's bed, a plastic bag of blood drains down through a tube.

The nurse sees me looking. She says, 'You're lucky.'

She can't have read my notes. I don't tell her I'm not lucky. I look at you instead. You're yawning just like a real person, looking into my eyes with a wondering expression, as if I am exactly the way you thought I'd be.

I touch each tiny curled finger with its perfect transparent fingernail. I stroke your black black hair.

5

'That'll rub off,' laughs the nurse. 'She'll be bald as an egg in a couple of weeks.'

I'm not listening. I've had a startling thought. 'It's my birthday!' I say. 'I just remembered.' I can't believe I almost forgot my own birthday.

The nurse sighs. 'Being a mother will do that to you. Another few months and you'll forget your own name.'

I'm still holding your finger. I want us to go on travelling down corridors like this for ever, never arriving and always always together like this.

They've fastened a plastic bracelet around your wrist. A label inside says BABY BIRD.

My baby bird, I think. My present from me to me.

Your eyelids glisten as if they've been smeared with Vaseline. I kiss them. You're my baby bird. My birthday present. My unforgettable sixteenth birthday present.

I open my eyes. The mad clattering of the trolley, the careering sensation stops dead. It's one year later and I'm in a motorway café. It's completely bland and im-personal, which is why I chose it. No one to notice a girl sitting too long over her empty cup.

I keep my eyes on my watch. The gold hand flicks flicks around the dial. Around me, people come and go, wiping tables, setting down trays.

Flash!

I jump. Someone must be taking photographs. But it's just a knife catching the sun. Next time I look at my watch it's 4.30 p.m. You're born! You're out there in the world with your beautiful blackbird hair; somewhere with pink balloons and a cake with one candle and teddy bears. You're born and I can hold you any time I like.

All I have to do is close my eyes.

Carrie-Anne

I often think that if Mum didn't have her 'schedule' gluing her together, she'd shatter like a glass. Sometimes I see the cracks under her exterior of control. As though she is a beautiful piece of tapestry but I can spy the loose threads and knots.

Beads of sweat are sliding down my dad's flushed cheeks as he awkwardly attempts to shift the refrigerator to its new home. My mum has been rearranging the furniture again.

'It's a breath of fresh air.' She sighs. 'Like a whole new house and not a penny spent.'

'No, just Dad's blood, sweat and tears,' I say accusingly, giving my dad's arm a comforting squeeze.

'Your father's just fine, Carrie-Anne. He enjoys doing little things for me. Don't you, sweetheart?'

My father's face has turned a deep shade of crimson. All

he can do is nod, puffing hard as he musters all his strength to give the fridge one final push.

'Mum, is Dad going to have a heart attack?' Robert giggles nervously.

'Don't be silly.' She gives Robert a reassuring pat on the head. 'Your father's as fit as he was when he was a young man.'

My stomach begins to churn at the way in which my mum sentimentally glances in my father's direction. The lack of authenticity makes me cringe. Fraud, I think to myself.

'Right! Time to go.'

My father has only just switched the fridge back on. 'What, now? Shouldn't I change my shirt first?'

'No time. I promised Tim we'd be there early to sort out refreshments.'

Every Thursday evening my parents go to an educational class. This year it is conversational Spanish; last year it was art appreciation. My mother clicks her fingers impatiently, commanding my dad's attention and submission. 'Come on. We don't want to be late for Tim.'

I roll my eyes and slump onto the terracotta-coloured sofa. 'Tim Shakespeare is such a wanker. You know he pervs

over the girls at school all the time. Ugh! And he looks like a slug. A big oversized, gross slug.'

'Carrie! Don't be so rude. He's a lovely man and he's been very good to you, helping you out with your school work.'

'You think he'd be so helpful if I wore my skirts a little longer?'

'You have a mucky mind, young lady. Those gutter thoughts won't make you any friends. Now make sure Robert, Emma and Sarah brush their teeth before bed. And no scary films.'

I grab the TV remote control and flick it on. When I am in this kind of mood, my defences are impenetrable.

Finally they are gone and I can breathe, finally let go of my resentful adolescent alter ego. I lope upstairs and pounce on my brother. 'Fancy a game of Monopoly, nappy head?'

On Thursday nights I can relax my scowl. I soften as I play make-believe with my siblings. I become a princess, a lion, a pirate. I travel the landscapes of my brother and sisters' imaginations, transported to a place, a time, where only we exist.

'I don't want to play.' Jelly Bean's lower lip begins to tremble. 'I never win. Even when you try and let me.'

'I know, we'll play in teams,' I suggest, wrapping my arms tightly around her. 'And you can be on my side — that way we can either win or lose together.'

This is the person I'd like to be. This is the person I could be.

Naomi

For six days I have the little four-bed ward to myself. The day before I have to leave they wheel in a young woman on a trolley. When the nurses have gone, she heaves herself, wincing, into a sitting position. She's just a girl, maybe my age, sixteen or seventeen. I see her glance at the cot beside her. A baffled expression flickers over her face as if she's wondering where the hell it came from.

I say tentatively, 'Hi, I'm Naomi.'

She blanks me, hunting in her locker for a comb, fussing with her hair. So far as she's concerned, she's alone. She ignores me until the night nurse dims the lights and the ward fills with its eerie green glow, the closest it ever gets to dark.

When I hear her voice I assume she's talking in her sleep. But apparently it's me she's talking to. About how her real dad died and her new dad knocked her about. 'Then I started seeing this boy and fell for a baby and Mum kicked me out. My boyfriend's coloured,' she adds nervously, as if I'll think badly of her for this.

Outside of old movies, I've never heard anyone say 'coloured' before.

'The social worker says he'll help me keep my little boy, but I've got to show I can keep it together. "Find a job and a little flat, see if you can keep it together, Louise," he says.'

Louise goes on, pouring out her grim life history until she's talked herself out, then she goes quiet. I don't think she's sleeping, she's just lying there, trying to make sense of it all. Suddenly she says in a dreamy voice, 'You know all those times you want to scream? Really scream at the top of your voice?'

'Yes,' I say very quietly.

'But you know you mustn't, so you swallow it down?'

I don't want to be listening to this. 'Yes,' I say again.

'Where do they go?' she asks me. 'Where do all those screams go?'

I don't answer. I don't tell her I've been wondering

something equally insane. Only it isn't screams I wonder about. It's this:

What happens to all that longing, the love you're supposed to give to someone, but you can't?

Where does it go?

Will it travel through the air, down telephone wires, across rail tracks, through walls to find you? Will it touch you while you sleep, like snowflakes or angel kisses? Will you feel it in your dreams, Maya?

I mean, all that love I feel for you, it can't just disappear.

Carrie-Anne

'Jelly Bean, I need to study! Leave that alone.'

I am chasing Emma around my room, but completely failing to retrieve my English homework.

'Read me a story,' she squeaks. 'Read me a story now!'

'I don't have time. I have exams.' I manage to grab her tiny body and throw her over my shoulder. 'You little monkey, give me back my book!'

I sit on my bed and Emma slips down beside me.

'Please, Carrie,' she whimpers softly.

Looking at her pale face and puppy-dog eyes, I decide to relent. 'OK, you go and get one of your books and you can read me a story.'

'Yay!' She leaps up and dashes out of the room.

I close my eyes and remember the painful conversation I've just had with my mum. Tears begin to well up in my eyes, but I scrunch them up tightly, refusing to let them flow. It's

my right to find my mum, to know where I come from, can't anyone understand that?

If I wasn't sixteen and angry, my mother's face would have destroyed me.

'But why, Carrie-Anne? Why would you want to see her? We're your family. We always have been.'

I couldn't explain. I couldn't explain the triumph I felt at making my mother cry. It made me angry that she didn't understand why.

'Because it's my right!' I wanted to explode. Years of pain swelled up in my gut, making me want to retch. 'Because Sarah looks like Aunt Suzy, Robert looks like Grandpa Harris, and beautiful, perfect little Emma is your clone. I have no face in this family. I want to know where my reflection comes from.'

It's like a Mexican stand-off: Mum at one end of the room, me at the other, our hands twitching by our sides ready to strike.

'How did you find her?'

'Dad's stuff.'

'That was private, Carrie-Anne. It wasn't meant for your eyes.'

'Then why did Dad look for her?'

Mum doesn't reply immediately. She seems to be struggling to decide what to do, what to say. She takes a deep breath and meets my questioning gaze.

'Because we thought when you were older, more mature, we'd give you her address and let you decide then.'

'I am older and more mature. What? Were you going to wait until I was dead?'

She moves towards me, arms outstretched. I duck away but her arms remain extended and frozen, then reluctantly drop as though heavy weights are connected to them.

'It was two years ago. After Great-Uncle Adam died. He left your father some money, and he decided to try and trace Naomi. We found her in Newquay. I thought it was a bad idea, but for once he was determined, and nothing I could say would change his mind. But you weren't meant to see it . . . not yet. Please, Carrie, think about it some more.'

'No. I've made up my mind.'

She goes quiet. No more arguing. No more tears. Just silence. Then she leaves the room. That's how much my mother loves me. She gets up and, without a word, leaves me.

I fall back onto my bed, imagining that the glow-stars on my ceiling are little planets, alternate realities.

In one my mystery mum is a superstar. Diamonds for breakfast, lunch and dinner. Her hair is gold. Her skin made of pearl.

In the next, a woman with a parade of mismatched children. There she stands amongst the litter and dog shit. My mother. Nicotine stained and punctured, mini train tracks running up her arm.

I make a promise to myself. A promise to find out which glow-star she lives on. Which alternate reality I missed out on.

I feel warm breath on my cheek and little Emma is beside me. She's my little Jelly Bean. She's all sticky jam hands and leaves sweet smudges on my skin. I think, Jelly Bean, when I find my real life, and my real name, and my real mother, I won't forget you.

I close my eyes and try to picture my mystery mum's face, in her mystery world.

Naomi

The stupid thing, the really stupid thing is, I was never going to be like my mother. Living with her is like being on a seesaw. You never know which way it's going to tip. When she's up it's party time. When she's down . . .

Some days I get stomach cramps just walking in the door, purely from the raw emotion swirling around our flat. That's before I've seen the smashed mugs, the cold coffee dripping down the walls . . .

Well, I'm not going to be like that. I'm not going to make my kids move home every few months just because (to pick a random example) I've foolishly slept with the guy in the top-floor flat, then found out he was a complete psycho.

My kids are going to have a real permanent home, with two real permanent parents and a fridge with real edible food; not a bottle of slimline tonic water, twelve reels of black and white film and half a rotting avocado.

There'll be no plate throwing, no coffee on the wall, no broken promises, no lies and absolutely *no* emotional blackmail.

I'm going to show my mum how a kid should be loved.

I'm going to be a real grown-up, not an overgrown teenager in disguise.

All I have to do is avoid Mum's mistakes.

That's all.

I've got two mothers, that's the problem. The moody, unpredictable person I live with most of the time. And the real one, the one I love. The mum who runs up an entire wardrobe of magical dressing-up clothes on her sewing machine, when asthma keeps me off school for weeks. The one who gets out of bed in the night when a freak storm cuts off our electricity, and bakes a huge lemon meringue pie by candlelight, turning the frightening power cut into some kind of crazy party.

In a way I have two dads too. The distant but basically decent man I lived with until I was six years old. And his image as officially relayed by my mother: Dr Death, the life-hating zombie.

'Naomi, he was killing my spirit! I've always loved life. I wanted him to love it too. I'd get holiday brochures and he'd say, "Allie, what *is* the point of going abroad? They've made everywhere the same! Why go all that way just to get food poisoning?"'

It's possible my father had some sort of personality change, though I can't say for sure. All I know is, after their divorce, he landed himself a job in America and never came back.

My mum should probably never have married Dad, but I think he must have acted as some kind of anchor, because those first few years after they split up, Mum and I seemed to be on the move non-stop. The pattern goes something like this:

For weeks at a time, our lives are blissfully normal. Regular school, more or less regular meals and bed times. Then Mum gets twitchy. I come to recognize the signs. She'll say, 'God! I'd like to know what I've done wrong, ending up in a hole like this.' And she'll go on about how it never stops raining in this godforsaken country. 'I'm an artist, I need light!' she tells everyone.

When my mother starts ranting about light, I take to

wandering around the flat with our little tabby cat clutched tightly to my chest.

Dizzy is the sweetest, funniest cat in the world. His whiskers are ridiculously big for his small pointy face. When he yawns, his furry jaws stretch into an elongated O, and his outsize whiskers vibrate like violin strings. At night, he creeps into my room and winds himself round me like a soft plushy scarf, filling my nostrils with fishy fumes and purring his squeaky purr until I fall asleep at last.

But any day now Dizzy and I will be parted. Mum will spring me from whichever school I'm attending at the time, and we'll trek off to stay with her old friends in Portugal or Italy or the south of France.

'I need sunlight!' she repeats to the taxi driver on the way to the station. 'I need heat! Without it, I die inside.'

I see now that Mum's furious craving for foreign heat and light stood for everything that's missing in her life. The wonderful man, the understanding friends, the perfect home. Her life had turned out like that dud puzzle I bought once at a jumble sale. It had a gorgeous picture on the box but when I opened it there were just meaningless bits of sky.

But as the train pulls out of the station, my mother's depression melts away like a bad dream. She produces treats to keep me entertained: finger puppets, lucky bags, colouring books, stick-on tattoos.

The other passengers exchange smiles and I am choked with pride. I've got my real mum back and I'd willingly keep travelling my entire childhood to stay in her company.

We arrive at our destination and Mum is like a girl on her honeymoon. She loves everything! The sun. The views. To her this unsanitary dump, her spaced-out friends and their unkempt hippy children represent heaven on earth. At this stage, the smell of bad drains, the pot of mouldy lentils no one bothers to throw away, the weird vibes between husband and wife don't even register.

Exhausted from the journey, I sleep in late, but Mum is up at sunrise, feverishly snapping pictures: sunflowers, gnarled old olive trees, Mediterranean light rays slanting through a doorway, a toothless old man tenderly holding a new-laid egg in his veiny old hands.

We catch a bus to the local market and return with

bags of exotic fruits and vegetables. They're so fresh that as we unpack them the kitchen glows with borrowed colour. 'No, let me cook,' my mum insists. 'I'm going to cook us all dinner!' She spends all afternoon chopping and simmering, cheerfully dirtying every pan and dish in the house.

The meal is a fabulous feast going on for hours. Little kids stay up past their bed times without getting cranky. Shy husbands tell hilarious stories. Disappointed wives turn up the stereo and dance to old sixties hits until they're breathless.

'You've made us so welcome. I don't know when I've had so much fun!' Mum carols.

'But it's all because of *you*,' they tell her.

'Your mother is incredible, Naomi,' someone invariably tells me. 'Bouncing back after her divorce, making a living out of her art. Aren't you proud of her?'

'Oh, yes,' I say eagerly, forgetting all the times I wish she'd just get a real job like other mothers.

This is as good as it gets. The highest point of the seesaw.

I suspect Mum is hoping that if she can just be sweet

and funny enough – play enough cute games with her friends' whiny little kids, listen to everyone's tedious troubles sympathetically enough – they'll, I don't know, *adopt* her or something and she won't need to live alone any more.

But this strategy is doomed from the start.

Mum thinks of herself as a 'people person', but in reality she can only function one-to-one.

It takes her a few days to find her latest soul mate, the artist wife, the misunderstood husband. But as soon as Mum has identified her target, she homes in like a heat-seeking missile. And *abracadabra!* The rules change. Now Mum has to spend every waking moment with this person or she'll die. The rest of us are mere obstacles between my mother and her happiness.

Starting with me.

When we reach this stage, the slightest change in my expression, even breathing too loud, can bring Mum down on me like the wrath of God.

'What *is* the matter with you, Naomi!' she rages. 'Oh, I get it! Mothers aren't allowed to have any fun, is that it? Christ! If I'd known you were going to be such a little misery, I'd have left you with your miserable bastard of a father. Serve you both right!'

When Mum starts finding fault like this, I get a wormy feeling in the pit of my stomach. Now it's going to happen for sure. Any minute now, something will tip the balance. Mum will overdo the sisterly sympathy, convince the artist wife that her husband is a monster, insanely jealous of her talent, or she'll go overboard with the female charm and end up in bed with the husband. Either way there'll be yelling and recriminations.

I have a memory of one grim-faced woman driving us to the station in the middle of the night, dumping us and our bags in the street and speeding off again with a furious squeal of tyres.

Details vary but one thing remains the same.

It ends. And we find ourselves on the train heading home.

On the return journey, Mum stares out of the window, her face pinched with disappointment. I droop in sympathy. But as the scenery becomes increasingly familiar; the clock tower, an abandoned hosiery mill, I feel a treacherous burst of joy. *I'm going home!* Tonight

I'll sleep on my own clean-smelling pillows. Drink tea out of my own mug. Best of all, I can start delicate diplomatic negotiations with Dizzy, so he'll forgive me for leaving him with strangers.

There's a line of taxis waiting outside the station. Bollywood film music blares from their radios. As our driver swings one-handed into the one-way system, past red-brick terraces and tiny corner shops, I sink back into the furry seat covers, with their smell of old cigarettes, and allow myself to breathe out properly for the first time in days.

'Did you have a good trip?' the taxi driver asks my mother.

'Fabulous!' she says immediately. 'But I was ready to come back.'

'Oh, yes,' he sighs. 'Home is where the heart is, isn't it?'

Carrie-Anne

Carl's snuck into our class. Now he and Gem are snuggled up at the back of the biology lab. They seem so immersed in each other that I am unsure where she begins and he ends. It is like a newly evolved being, with two heads and two hearts.

Gem and I formed an uneasy alliance back in Year Ten. Mum often refers to her as my 'misunderstood' friend, and OK, she's not the easiest person to be around, but we always manage to have a laugh. Most of the girls at school call her the 'Borderline Bitch', or right-out cow, depending on how much trouble she's been causing. Until she met Carl, nicking other people's boyfriends was her favourite pastime. I sometimes forget that I'm the one who intro-duced Carl to Gem. He'd been mates with Matt for ages. We'd been like the three musketeers, going forth and making mischief. Now that Gem's on board Dad calls us the Four Horsemen of the Apocalypse.

Mr Clarkson, the substitute teacher, still hasn't found his missing notes. We only have half an hour of dissection left.

Matt is in a corner conducting 'business'. He has been my world as far back as I can remember. I can't imagine a Matt-free world. Not having him just round the corner, a few paces behind, right next to me. He is my soul mate and my saviour.

He raps on my forehead with his rough knuckles. 'Planet Earth to Space Cadet Harris. Hello! Is anyone there?'

'Ouch, you arse-hole. That hurt!' I squeal.

Everyone around me is pairing off like the animals going into the ark two by two. I've actually had a huge, silly crush on Gemma's Carl for years but I never had the guts to take the risk and tell him, and now it's too late and he's with Gemma. Since Carl vanished from my radar of possible mates, I've begun to see Matt in a whole new light. I'm still not sure if he sees me as anything more than a friend, but I'm willing to find out.

Mr Clarkson thinks he has left his notes in what he calls the faculty lounge. With a speedy superman exit, he's gone.

'So, you up for doing something interesting on Friday night?'

I love Matt's propositions. You know from the glint in his

eyes that in his world 'interesting' means dangerous, bad and fun. But I'm not going to let him know about the million butterflies that have invaded my belly, or that my heart is in danger of breaking out of my chest.

'What kind of interesting? If you hadn't already noticed, we live in a fun-free zone.'

Matt is busy stocktaking, hands moving cautiously, slowly, under the table. White, pink and baby-blue pills, aluminium squares, lumps of greenery wrapped in cling film.

'Well, darlin'. I was thinking we haven't as yet celebrated your birthday. Not in style anyway. My mate Andy has us down on the guest list at Chaos.'

My heart stops. I am officially dead. 'Chaos! That's in London! Are you insane? How?'

Matt just taps his nose. A long-established gesture that means, Don't ask, just be there.

'Are Gemma and Carl in on this?'

But Matt has turned away to conduct more business. The dreadlocks his father painstakingly twisted with beeswax are now shaven. His head is as naked as a newborn's. But the eyes haven't altered. His pupils are perpetually dilated, the

irises the colour of jade, his stare unflinching and uncompromising.

'Hey, you. What's going on?' Gemma slumps beside me on one of the hard wooden lab stools. 'Carl's gone back to the common room. Carrie, things are really bad between us at the moment!'

Gem rests her head on my shoulder, sticking her bottom lip out like a petulant child. 'I think Carl's getting bored of me. He says I suffer from "severe mood swings". What the fuck is that supposed to mean? Remind me why I even bother going out with a seventeen-year-old.'

'Because you said that the boys in our year were un-sophisticated cheapskates. Anyway, guess what? We're off to Chaos on Friday night.' I can't suppress a wide grin. 'I'm so excited. Matt is such a sweetie.'

'It was Carl's idea – Matt was all set for a few pints at the Three Nuns.' Gemma has a natural ability to piss on my parade.

'The Three Nuns! Cheapskate! That's such a skanky pub.' I'd let myself believe Matt's party plans were some kind of acknowledgement of his true feelings for me, a sign from the universe that he might just love me.

'Yeah, but the Nuns is a great place for business – all those crusty, arty types with Mummy and Daddy's money to burn.' Gemma begins to comb her fingers through her hair. 'I can't believe he's still dealing after last year's fuck-up. You'd think six months banged up inside would . . . I don't know, put him off.'

'It was young offenders, not prison. There is a difference.' I'm beginning to get annoyed with Gemma's tendency to tell anyone who is willing to listen that Matt was sent down for drug possession the previous year. Like somehow by association, she too is unpredictable, a risk taker, a wild child.

'I mean, I think I'd shoot myself – or at least shoot someone, if I had to repeat this year again.' Gemma takes a silver compact out of her bag and starts to study her reflection. 'Do you think I over-pluck my eyebrows?'

I begin to scribble over all the hearts I've been doodling in my notebook. 'What answer did you get for question four?'

'You're kidding, right?' Gemma snaps her compact shut, grabs my books and shoves them into my bag. 'Let's ditch this afternoon's lesson and go shopping. We'll only be discussing that Anne Frank film in English class anyway.'

'Book. *The Diary of Anne Frank* is a book.'

'Whatever – did you see how skinny she got in the last episode?'

'That would be because she was in a concentration camp.'

'Yeah, well, all I can say is, Lucky thing. I'd love to be that skinny.'

I look at Gemma in disbelief.

'What? What did I say? God, do I have something on my face?'

'No. Um, yeah, sure, let's go shopping.'

'Excellent! We'll go to the Blissbar and have our nails done! I'll just send Carl a text and tell him to meet us later.'

I suddenly feel lighter, almost happy. If only for a few moments I can forget about the constant arguing with my mother. And on Friday night I will party until my body is crippled and my breath has gone. I will wail like a banshee and live again.

Naomi

Living with my mother is like the fortune-telling game where you pull petals off little daisies. 'She loves me, she loves me not, she loves me . . .'

It's not a nice thing to say, but my mother abandons me on a regular basis. Whenever someone more exciting comes along in fact. She'll strike up a conversation with some female stranger in a doctor's waiting room and before you know it, they're on the phone every night, exchanging mind-bogglingly intimate histories, slagging off their selfish kids and clueless ex-husbands. I have to hum loudly as I cross our hallway, so as not to hear what she really thinks of me.

But like the Little Match Girl waiting to come in from the cold, I hang on. That's because I know something Mum's exciting new friends and lovers don't.

Sooner or later they'll all fail her. They'll fail her big-time. And then she'll need me.

The humiliating thing is that I'm grateful. I get home from school and instantly I'm little Florence Nightingale, fetching Mum's migraine pills, shutting out the world behind her bedroom curtains, laying cool cloths on her hot forehead. I stroke her hand timidly while she tosses and turns.

And sometimes it actually happens, the thing I'm longing for.

My mother sees me, really sees me. She pulls me into her arms, hugging me so hard I can't breathe. 'My little pearl,' she says brokenly. 'I think you're the only person who really understands.'

I hold her as she sobs and my heart swells with what I genuinely believe is happiness.

I never notice the exact moment that Mum and I swap places. When did she get to be the child, causing mayhem, while I'm stuck with playing responsible adult? Hiding her cigarettes so she won't die of cancer and leave me an orphan, reminding her to eat when she's depressed. Getting up in the night to check she remembered to lock the door.

Yet strange as it seems, our bizarre trade seems to work. Gradually Mum starts acting proud of me. She even shows me off to her current girlfriend.

'Do you know what Naomi did last night?' she coos. 'I got back late from taking pictures at the women's peace camp. I was soaked, absolutely gibbering with cold, and this little angel ran me a hot bath. Did you ever hear of anything so sweet? And when I got out, she had my supper waiting!' Mum beams at me through swirls of cigarette smoke.

Her friend nods sagely. 'She's a Capricorn, isn't she?'

'But I think my moon is in Aries, isn't it, Mum?' I chip in.

Now that I'm an honorary grown-up, I've started joining in adult conversations, delivering witty comments with a worldly smile. Most times I have *no* idea what I'm talking about, and anyone with half a brain would tell me to push off and play with my Sindy doll, but Mum is totally taken in.

She's not the only one. As time goes by, I genuinely believe this middle-aged nine-year-old spouting gobbledegook is actually me. Faking it is my ticket into Mum's magic circle. So I go on faking it for all I'm worth.

When I'm not being a fake adult, I do a tolerable impersonation of a child. Any time I get off from being my mother's minder, I skip off to play with Anna or Rachel or Emma, depending on where Mum and I are living at the time.

Together my little friends and I put on puppet shows, build camps in the garden and go to each other's birthday treats. We have great times. I know this is true, because I have the photographs to prove it.

But I'm like a paramedic at a party, afraid to relax in case my beeper goes off and I have to be summoned back to base.

There seems to be a clause in our invisible mother–daughter contract which reads something like this: Having fun without Mum is acceptable if, and only if, my mother is off somewhere having even *more* fun. Otherwise it's an act of treachery.

Once I make a really stupid mistake.

A new girl called Verity Meadows comes to my school. Her parents own some kind of family business and make pots of money. For some reason Verity takes to me. Despite the money and the big house, I think she's almost as lonely as me. She seems touchingly grateful when I accept her invitation to sleep over, subject to my mother's approval.

I run to find Mum as soon as I get home. Her studio door is open, so I know it's OK to go in. She's looking at a batch of prints pegged up on a little plastic washing line. After Mum develops her negatives she often spends weeks playing with images, enlarging, cropping, editing out anything that doesn't fit the perfect picture she has inside her head.

This afternoon she seems listless and preoccupied. When I ask if I can sleep over at Verity's tomorrow, she just sighs, 'If you want.' I notice this lack of enthusiasm, but I assume she's getting one of her headaches.

Next morning I pack my overnight bag, tiptoe past her bedroom so as not to disturb her and close the front door behind me.

After school, Verity and I walk back together to her home. I've never been in a genuinely rich person's house before. I'm dazzled by their fridge crammed with child-friendly snacks. Most of all I'm impressed with her bedroom ceiling, which features a huge glittering map of the night sky.

'I love outer space,' Verity tells me. 'I'm going to be an astronaut when I grow up.'

I shudder. 'That would be too scary for me.'

'It wouldn't, Naomi, because they'd train you,' she explains earnestly.

We spend the evening wafting around Verity's house in slow motion, being astronauts in outer space. For the first time in my life I forget all about my mother and have a wonderful time.

Next morning I let myself into the flat, desperate to ask Mum if I can paint stars and planets on my ceiling too.

'Mum!' I sing out. 'Mummy, where are you?'

She doesn't answer.

I find her in her studio, staring at a heap of bills – gas, phone, electricity. She's sitting so still that I go cold inside.

'Mum?' I say timidly.

My mother jumps up and barges past me as if I'm

invisible. I hear her crashing into the kitchen like a drunk, filling the kettle, slamming cupboard doors. *Slam! Slam!*

I trail after her. 'What did I—?'

A sharp intake of breath, practically a hiss, and then Mum goes crazy, hurling crockery, screaming.

I betrayed her. I'm a snake in the grass, like my father. A selfish little cow, only thinking of myself. I *knew* how scared she was, all these bills to pay, no money coming in, yet I went *swanning* off to my rich friend without giving her a second thought . . .

I don't know how long it goes on, but it feels like a lifetime.

Later, we cry into each other's hair and say we're sorry. I help her sweep up the mess. Later still, Mum finds a fiver she forgot about in her coat pocket. We go out in the dark to buy a Chinese takeaway and rent a video and spend the evening cuddling on the sofa. We're like earthquake victims, shocked, shaky and kind of awed. But it's over, and it will never happen again.

A few days later Verity invites me to stay over next

weekend. 'We can play astronauts again!' she says earnestly.

I feel a physical jolt as if I've run up against an invisible electric fence. 'I can't,' I say. 'Sorry.'

Carrie-Anne

I look at my mum and try to remember when she began to irritate me so much. One minute she was the most important thing in my life, my anchor. Next thing I knew, I could hardly bear to be in the same room. The way her mouth crinkles in the corners. The way she clicks her fingers, as though I am a misbehaving dog, makes me want to plunge a kitchen knife into her back. I feel guilty about having these violent thoughts. I worry that I am secretly psychotic, just waiting for that one thing that will knock me over the edge. That final something that will drive me to the top of a high building with a shotgun.

I finish applying my lip liner and survey the face of a nutter! It is the big night. The night we are going to Chaos. And bizarrely enough, my mum is busy ironing my trousers for the occasion. This just makes me resent her even more. I know she is sad, but I don't care. I think she envies my youth. My slim hips and concave stomach. She used to be beautiful. I'd watch her brush her hair and I'd think there was no one who compared to her. Her skin was like fine silk and I'd stroke her cheek, trying to imagine what else could feel as delicate and perfect. Gradually her skin began to sag and her hair lost its shine. Now my eyes are the ones that sparkle and my skin is soft and supple. I watch her slow movements and I grind my teeth. I watch as in triple slow motion she places the iron on the sideboard, then with annoying accuracy folds my trousers.

'There you are, darling. All done.'

I shrug my shoulders. 'Whatever.'

'Say thank you, Carrie-Anne.'

I turn and see my father standing in the doorway, wiping his hands on a tea towel. My mother rushes over to him, yanks the towel out of his hand and shakes it accusingly in his face.

'What did I tell you? Don't wipe that dirty car oil on the tea towels!'

I can't believe how she speaks to my father. Like he is one of her children. An extra person to patronize. My mother's coping mechanism is to diminish. Whenever life gets too

hard or she feels like she is losing control, she just under-mines whoever is nearest and dearest.

'Dad! Don't let her talk to you like that. She's not your mother.'

I realize I've 'crossed the line'. I've been fuelling my mum's frustration towards me all day. Poking and prodding, ignoring her requests, pretending not to hear her feeble attempts at small talk. I've pushed and pushed and now I can see the cracks appear.

'She! Her!' My mother spits out these words like a rattlesnake. 'Carrie, I am so sick of that snide mouth of yours. It's just too tiring having to put up with your crap. Stop it.'

My father and I are stunned. Mum never swears. My father shuffles his feet. I know he is about to exit this uncomfortable scene. I am trying to keep my cool. I tell myself I don't want a huge blow-up before my birthday party.

I turn back to the mirror and adjust my hair, mumbling, 'Someone needs some extra hormones. Hello, can we say "the menopause"?'

That's all it takes.

'What did you say, young lady?'

My father doesn't even pretend to search for an excuse – he just leaves the room.

'God! I was only joking. Chill out already.' I'm not going to let her get to me, ruin another special moment for me.

'Well, maybe you should go to your room and think about how you're going to apologize for your little joke.'

'You're going to send me to my room! But I'm sixteen—'

'This is my house! And while you live here under my roof you will obey my rules.'

I shrug my shoulders. 'I wonder if you'll expect your *real* children to *obey* you when they're older? Anyway, I'm not looking for a fight, Mum. Can we leave this, for God's sake?' I touch up my lips with pink, frosty gloss. 'I mean, really, could you be any more uncool?'

My mum is folding up the ironing board. 'I don't know why I bother, Carrie-Anne. Why do you insist on behaving like a smug little cow so much of the time? We used to have fun – do you remember that?'

I choose not to remember and make no response.

My mum sighs. It isn't disapproving or disappointed. It is

real and full of pain. 'There doesn't seem to be anything your father or I can do about it. Just go.'

Later, when we are sitting on the train to London, I think about the way Mum looked when she told me to leave. She seemed completely deflated, as though the air had been punched out of her. It isn't like I want to make life complicated for my family. It just seems to happen that way. I start off with genuinely good intentions, but sooner or later I am storming out of the room, slamming every door that gets in my way. My life seems to be littered with words I never have the guts to say. All the 'I love you's just hanging there in space waiting to find a place, a time where they belong.

Gem winks at me. 'Hey, Boo. What are you thinking about?'

'Nothing interesting.'

'Get it together, girl. We're about to go to *the* most slammin' club in London.'

'Slammin'? You have to stop watching that American teen crap. I am trying to get all excited, but I'm so tired. It's like every single day my mum has to find something to bitch about. It's doing my nut. I'm seriously worried I'm about to crack.'

Gem rolls her eyes. 'Carrie, Carrie. That's what they're supposed to do. They nag and we give them reasons to!'

'I guess you're right.'

'You know it. Now, how about a nice drink to steady your nerves?' She produces a bottle of what looks like innocent lemonade. She unscrews the cap. 'Don't worry, it packs a punch.'

I take a long hard swig. 'God, Gem, how much vodka did you put in this? It tastes like something my dad would use to clean his paintbrushes.'

Gemma begins to pick furiously at her nail varnish.

'What's up?'

'Carl and I have been at each other's throats for the past few weeks. It's non-stop now. I don't know why it's not working. It's just not fun any more.'

What can I say? Part of me wishes Carl would cut Gem loose. I hadn't had the guts to tell him how I felt until it was too late and he'd been snapped up. Gem and I believe in the best friend code of honour. Past, present and possibly future guys are out of bounds. All I can do is my duty and support my gal pal.

'Gem, I'm sure it's just a phase. Maybe you should just chill

out more. The one thing I do know about Carl is that he needs his space. Just hang in there; it will sort itself out.'

'You really think so?'

'Absolutely. Where are the guys anyway?' I stand up and look down the empty carriage.

Gemma stands up too. 'No doubt getting happy in the smoking carriage. I'll go and find them.'

I am glad I have friends like Matt, Gem and Carl. I don't think I'd have survived my mother without them. No matter how she criticizes me, they are there to pick me up. I lose a little piece of my mother each day, and our bond becomes more fractured with every moment we spend together. I am looking forward to Chaos: like my life it is an out-of-control place to be. I am looking forward to losing myself in the music, the hard, gut-thumping beats.

Like most things you spend every moment of every day looking forward to, Chaos is a big disappointment. The residue of the argument I've had with Mum just won't shake off. It feels cold and heavy like an iceberg lodged in my stomach.

'It's like I love him so much I don't want to lose him. That's why I don't tell him how I feel. See?'

We are in the queue for the toilets; Gem is talking to a girl whose face is stained with a mixture of black mascara and blue eye shadow.

'I love him so much, but that makes me weak. He has the power to hurt me, whenever he likes. See?'

Gem nods enthusiastically. 'I know exactly what you mean. It's like with Carl. Say one word about how you feel and he's out the door.'

The girl wobbles slightly and puts her hand on Gem's shoulder. 'Is Carl your husband?'

'God no!' Gem giggles. 'I'm only sixteen.'

The girl shakes her head, loses her balance and topples onto the floor. 'Fuck! I'm taking advice from a sixteen-year-old. I'm twenty-five and I'm listening to you?'

We help her to her feet. Before we can get her standing steady on her four-inch pointy heels, she's fallen over again, dragging us with her. That's my life. I always end up sitting in other people's crap, stale beer, cigarette butts and chewing gum stuck to my arse.

Naomi

I'm like a girl on hurricane duty, watching for danger signs. The slightest change in Mum's tone puts me on red alert. Next thing it'll be 'God I hate this place – not enough room to swing a cat; how can I work, if I can't even breathe?' And we'll be on a train heading south.

One wet Sunday, Mum comes out of her studio with a batch of ruined negatives and dumps them in the bin. I hear her draw a deep breath.

I know I have to move fast. She's going to start on her 'I need sun, I need inspiration' speech. I can already hear her saying the words in my head.

'Mum, you look really pale,' I say daringly. 'You need some fresh air. Let's go for a walk. We could go down by the canal.'

'Naomi, why the hell would I want to go for a walk? It's *peeing* down out there. In case you've forgotten, I'm supposed to be getting pictures ready for this sodding exhibition.'

'You could take your camera,' I suggest. 'You could take pictures and get some fresh air at the same time.'

Amazingly, she agrees. She even gives me a hug. 'You funny child,' she says. 'You're like a prim little old lady sometimes.'

Mum tosses me my raincoat, still laughing, and we set off towards the canal. Her smile quickly fades.

There are slugs on the towpath, outsized slimy ones the colour of cold tea, and we have to watch where we tread. The air is rank with the smells of nettles and dogs. People have dumped all this junk in the water – bits of rusty pram and polystyrene packaging. We walk along past blind-looking ruins of old factory buildings, and my heart sinks.

Did I really think a walk by some skanky canal could compensate my mother for her shitty going-nowhere single-parent life?

I hunch my shoulders miserably, waiting for her to order me home to pack my bags.

Then, quite without warning, something beautiful

happens. The rain eases off. The clouds part. And miraculous ladders of light stream down.

'Oh, that is just . . .' Mum fumbles for her camera. 'Just *look* at that,' she whispers to herself, and all at once she's snapping away like a demon.

I practically have to drag her home to tea.

That night she's still got clouds on the brain. I hear her playing the old Joni Mitchell song, 'Both Sides Now', while I'm in the bath.

I'm just drifting off to sleep when Mum puts her head round my door. She's washed her hair and I can smell the scent of her shampoo. 'I just wanted to tell you that you're amazing, Naomi,' she says softly. 'Funny, special and completely amazing.'

Mum's new obsession lasts for months. Every chance she gets, she's out of doors photographing clouds. She tells me the names of all their different formations – cirrus, cumulus, nimbus . . .

It's like she's reciting poetry.

Every day she tacks up her latest efforts. Her studio comes alive with airy presences.

Sometimes I wander into the studio just to look at

them. I sit on the floorboards cross-legged, inhaling the smell of developing fluid, not really knowing why I'm here. I've never been interested in Mum's work before, but these pictures move me in a way I can't express. For the first time I sense why someone might want to be an artist.

One night Mum goes out to her women's group and comes back with a curly-haired woman in floaty ethnic trousers. My mother seems excited, almost shy, as she introduces her.

'Naomi, this is Lily Macsweeny. She wanted to see my clouds.'

'Tell the truth, I insisted,' the woman says, smiling.

I decide Lily is the palest woman I have ever seen. If you put her in the dark she'd light up like a glow star.

They go off to the studio and I hear Lily gasp. 'They've got so much energy. It's as if you've caught them just as they're about to change into something else.'

My mother sounds pleased. 'That's kind of what I was aiming for.'

I feel the balance shift, like an invisible shutter coming down. I'm not funny or special any more. I'm just in the

way. I unhook a sleepy Dizzy from the sofa and cart him
off to bed.

I lie hugging him tightly in the darkness. I don't want
to listen to their stupid conversation but my bedroom is
right next door to the studio, and so, against my will, I
find out all about Lily Macsweeny. Like Mum, she's a
single mother, and lives alone with her two daughters.
Like Mum, she lives from hand to mouth, earning money
doing aromatherapy massage and reflexology.

They move across to the kitchen. I hear Mum uncork
a bottle of wine and the atmosphere changes. They start
talking in an annoying female code. Mysterious phrases
float across my bed like cartoon speech bubbles.

'So how old were you?'

'Eighteen and totally clueless. How about you?'

'Twenty,' says Mum. 'Ditto.'

'Wouldn't be without them though, would you?' Lily
says.

There's a long pause and I quickly pull my pillow over
my head before I can hear the answer.

Just when everything was finally coming right, I'm
going to lose her to luminous Lily.

Carrie-Anne

'The merest of gestures is all it takes. In that one simple movement we know that he has completely broken her spirit, snatched away any semblance of dignity . . . possibly her humanity.'

In these moments I am mesmerized by my father. His eyes become bright and focused. It's as though something else has taken possession of his listless body and made it animated. He loves film. It is his escape into a world crammed with all kinds of possibilities and outcomes. Anything can, and probably will, happen. This mutual hunger for an exit from life is our bond. Our morphine hit, a momentary break from the pain of living.

'Do you see what I mean, Carrie?'

His gangly six-foot-three frame is stretched out full-length on the sofa. I crouch on the floor, an eager pupil desperate to know more. In these moments I too am alive, unafraid.

'You see it's not about strutting around, wringing one's hands in grief. It is the slightest of gestures that lets us know how deep and significant her pain is. A good director understands that it is the unspoken that gives a film its depth. Here, Carrie, we witness a master of direction at work.'

I nod enthusiastically. Why can't my father be this way all the time? A door key turns in the lock and he crumples his body into half its size, now only taking up a small proportion of the sofa. My mum angrily stumps into the living room.

'Carrie, get off the floor. This isn't a squat. What have you two been up to?'

My father returns to his usual state of vacancy. No one's at home.

'Just watching movies,' I answer.

'How nice. While I've been out doing the weekly shop, you've been watching television. How productive of you both.'

I can't tell whether her resentment is aimed at my father or me, or maybe both of us.

'Well? Don't just sit around like couch potatoes, come and help me with the bags. Oh, and Derek, in half an hour you'll have to pop round to Susan's to pick up the kids. Come on, chop chop.'

My father scrambles to his feet, catches his foot in the rug and stumbles. My mother tut-tuts as she leaves the room. He turns and gives me a sheepish grin before following her out to the car. With the merest of gestures he is gone.

Naomi

Lily drops by one Saturday afternoon, with a bottle of scented oil for Mum. She's brought her daughters Ruby and Kumara.

We eye each other warily. I know from my eaves-dropping that Kumara's dad was Asian and Ruby's was white. I notice with envy that they both have long, mermaidy hair. Ruby's is honey-brown; Kumara's inky blue-black.

Despite having a luminous white mother given to nose studs and shalwar kameez, the Macsweeny girls seem surprisingly normal.

I like them. I like them a lot. I shyly offer to make us all popcorn. Even though it isn't strictly necessary, all three of us hang onto the pot lid. When I see our joined hands, I start to smile, I don't know why.

Ruby is pretending to be scared, shrieking and pulling

dramatic faces as the corn kernels explode inside the pan.

'She's such a child,' says Kumara smugly.

We end up munching in front of the TV, howling with laughter at *The Dukes of Hazzard*, while our mums chat in the kitchen.

In a matter of days, the Macsweeny and Bird contingents have merged into one big happy single-parent family, with two mums and two addresses. I relinquish my lonely only status without a backward look.

Lily Macsweeny is very good news and I know it. When our flat is sold over our heads, it's Lily who helps us find a new place, a narrow terraced house with a courtyard, practically a garden. I run around with Lily's girls, our shoes echoing on the floorboards, as we peer excitedly into rooms. I'm wearing Kumara's pink and turquoise friendship bracelet on my ankle. I'm also trying to grow my hair, but it's taking for ever.

'There's an attic with a skylight!' I yell down to Mum.

Lily and Mum follow us up to the second floor.

'Hey, look,' says Lily, pointing at the sky. 'A live cloud installation!'

'I can smell damp,' says Mum doubtfully. 'Ugh, and those colours!'

'It needs some TLC, that's all. A lick of paint and you won't recognize it. You've even got a corner shop, did you see?'

On our way home we stop off at the cramped little grocery store and Lily buys us sherbet flying saucers. The sign over the shop originally said 'BALMORAL MINIMART', but the first three letters have gone missing. This sends Mum and Lily into fits of laughter. It might actually be the Moral Minimart which finally clinches the deal.

On moving day, Lily ropes in a friend with a van and helps us move our stuff. When the lick of paint turns out to use our whole week's grocery money, Lily feeds us at her house, until the financial emergency blows over.

Over macaroni cheese, we swap tales of hard times.

'We lived on lentils and potatoes for a whole month once, didn't we, Naomi?' says Mum.

'One time all we had in the cupboard was two slices of bread and an egg,' I say proudly. 'We just had eggy fried bread for supper.'

Lily wins this contest hands down. 'I used to make this *loaf* out of left-over porridge,' she tells us.

Mum gulps. 'Porridge bread? That sounds awful.'

'I *loved* it!' Ruby's eyes are shining. 'I'm always asking Mum to make it again, but she won't.'

Summer comes. There's no money for holidays, but somehow our mothers shoehorn all five of us into Mum's ancient blue 2 CV and take us off for days out.

I'm so happy chatting to Kumara and Ruby in the back that I totally forget to keep tabs on Mum and Lily in the front. Anyway, Kumara complains that they always talk about the same things. Men and S.E.X.

Now that I've stopped feeling responsible for fixing Mum's problems single handed, our mothers' disgusting female anecdotes and mad shrieks of laughter just form the comforting backing track to our own more exciting conversations.

Kumara and Ruby have got me hooked on old *Wonder Woman* repeats. The three of us are currently reinventing ourselves as the invincible Wonder Girls, just one of many reasons I'm desperate to grow my hair.

As I parade around back home in my home-made

cape, my bullet-deflecting cuffs and a magical lariat
made from Lily's dressing-gown cord, I have a new and
heady feeling.

I belong.

It's weeks now since I crept out of my room in the
night to make sure the back door is safely locked.

All those months we spent searching for paradise. And
now it's come and ambushed us in our own home town.

Carrie-Anne

Matt is going to get the car. That's the plan. Gemma and Carl want to hold my hand. Everyone wants a chunk of my drama, my journey, my adventure in Newquay. Mine. I'm not sure they even mean well, know what it's about. All they imagine is surf, sea and sand. And the weathermen are convinced we'll get sun. But I know that the heat of the sun won't be able to thaw the coldness I feel inside, the iciness my mum's silence has left. She hasn't spoken to me since I told her I wanted to find my real mum.

I try to broach the subject of going to Newquay in the most adult way possible. It is never going to be easy. She's barely said a full sentence to me since the night I went to Chaos. I make her a mug of coffee, a peace offering to show I'm grown-up enough to swallow my pride. The smile she gives me does nothing to encourage my newfound sensitivity. It's just a little too smug; it reads, 'I knew you'd

apologize sooner or later.' As if her punishing silences have somehow convinced me that she is right and I am bad for wanting to know where I come from. I have nothing to apologize for and she is going to see that.

'Mum, over Easter, Gem and I thought we'd take a few days off. Go on holiday.'

Silence.

'A kind of ritual, rites-of-passage thing. Before exams.'

Silence.

'Is that OK . . .?'

'Do you need my permission now? I thought as you'd turned sixteen you would be going your own way. Doing your own thing. Do you need my approval?'

Why is it that when mothers 'take that tone', they're being reasonable, caring, maternal? I speak like that and I am a little bitch, ungrateful.

She cuts me and has absolutely no idea how I bleed. My belly is full, a haemorrhaging of hate. She twirls my life like a spinning top, until I have no bearings. She is my mother, my compass, yet she refuses to let me find home. We dance around each other, reaching and retracting. She is sitting in our special place. The rocking chair, where I would snuggle up on her lap while she read me fairy tales. Now, arms that were once open to embrace me are folded tightly across her chest.

'No, I don't need your approval. I don't need your permission. I just thought you'd like to know my plans. That's all.'

'How thoughtful. Where are you going?'

'The seaside.'

'At this time of year?'

'We're going to Newquay.'

She stops. She knows my plans. Until this point, I truly believe my mother thought me to be head-to-toe bluff.

'You can't see her! She'll hurt you all over again!'

My bullshit detector springs into action. I know this isn't authentic concern for me.

'She won't want to see you. Carrie-Anne, love, wait until you're older. Those little tender bits less exposed.'

Her voice has turned all nurturing. But she remains fixed to the spot, the opposite side of the room to me, hands clenched.

That's how I know the words mean nothing. She wants me to stay, to prove her control. Maybe if she'd hold me, stroke my hair, touch my cheek, I would stay. She can hold

me any time, my mother, but she doesn't.

'Anyway, Mum, I'll be gone for ten days. I'll use Grandma's money.'

'That's for university!'

I don't argue; tell her that this is more important than higher education. I hesitate by the door. I dare not ask the question I really need the answer to. I dare not ask her, If I leave, can I return? She is my mother, this is my home and I want to come back. As I open the door I close my eyes and wait for the banishment. The 'If you leave this house, you will never be welcome here again.' But she keeps her punishing silence. And for the first time in days I am thankful.

Naomi

'Open your mouth, angel,' commands Lily. 'That's it.'

She drips two careful drops of Rescue Remedy under my tongue.

Mum had to whiz off on some big photographic assignment so Lily is looking after me. Unfortunately I got carried away during a Wonder Girls adventure and cracked my head on the kitchen doorstep.

After the Rescue Remedy, Lily gives me arnica tablets to suck.

'I wonder why you hurt yourself like that,' she says in a musing voice.

'Maybe she's missing her mum,' suggests Ruby.

To the Macsweenys nothing is ever accidental, not even an accident. A chance meeting, a bad cold, cutting your finger while you're slicing onions, these are all messages from your soul. You simply have to figure out what it's trying to tell you. I've learned heaps of things since Mum became friends with Lily. For example, angels aren't make-believe like fairies, they're real. Lily saw one in her kitchen when she was pregnant with Kumara. Also you don't have only the one life, you have thousands. That's why when you meet some people for the first time, you feel like you already know them.

Mum and Lily are positive they've met in at least one other life. A local psychic told them they used to be temple dancers in ancient times.

Maybe that's true, because one, two, then three years go by and they're still as thick as thieves.

Without quite noticing, I stop waiting for things to go wrong.

Usually I'm just starting to like Mum's friends when there's some hideous showdown and they're airbrushed from our lives for ever. I have to guard my tongue in case their names slip out by accident. And if Mum happens to bring them up first, I have to be careful that I only remember the bad things about them.

But Lily Macsweeny is different. She and Mum do have occasional fallings out but Lily always finds a way to patch things up. When Mum gets into one of her crash-and-burn moods, Lily says, 'But look how much you *learned* from that experience, Allie. Since I've known you, you've really grown as a person.'

It's true. Mum's growing so fast, she's even trying to be a vegetarian. Not only that, when she starts feeling stressed she takes deep breaths and practises the calming yoga poses Lily taught her.

Lily has explained to Mum that instead of problems, we should say 'challenges'. 'It's a different frame of mind,' she beams. 'When you have problems, you're a cosmic victim. When you meet challenges, you're a hero!'

Lily is constantly reading self-help books. One day she buys a paperback called *How to Create Your Own Reality*. She stays up all night reading it from cover to cover. The ideas in the book make her so excited, she wakes my mother up at seven in the morning to tell her about it.

Lily is convinced that if they both do everything the book says, our two families will soon be living lives completely free from worry and financial struggle.

Mum is instantly sold on this idea. Even though we are in a lentil and potatoes phase, she rushes out to buy her own copy, so she can create her reality without further delay.

That night she and Lily sit writing out positive statements called affirmations. *I am now attracting the perfect man for me. Miracles are natural. Now is the only time there is.*

Kumara and I write affirmations too. With our pink woolly leg warmers wrinkling around our ankles, we affirm that we are going to go to the New York School of the Performing Arts, where we plan to dance crazily on top of taxis like the kids in *Fame*.

I'm so excited I feel as if I might faint. This is just like Luke Skywalker learning to harness the Force! I've always secretly believed in magic. Now my faith has been rewarded. Life has turned into a beautiful fairytale.

Carrie-Anne

Gem helps me pack. Like real grown-ups we discuss ensembles. My travel bags bob up and down, a hyperactive Jelly Bean bouncing furiously on my bed. Whenever there is tension at home, Emma becomes manic. Like her extra energy will somehow compensate for the lack of love in the house. She begins to force her tiny body into one of my bags, jeans and T-shirts flying everywhere.

'Jelly Bean, stop it!'

Gem drags my little sister up by the ankles, swinging her like a giggling pendulum. But her eyes have a constant questioning: 'Why don't you love us any more?' She's been by my side incessantly since I told Mum about the trip. My miniature shadow. Clinging until my circulation stops. There is nothing I can say. Nothing that will make her understand that I'll come back. All I can do is donate my treasured Paddington Bear; ask her to foster it until I return. Even at

five, she can see it is just stuffing and fake fur. I can't give her my heart for safekeeping. What can I do?

Gem insists I pack every item of club-wear I possess. I don't have the heart to tell her the last thing I want to wear is a silver boob tube. Ever since my party at Chaos, Gem has been bitten by a big bug called hard house. Wherever we are, we are accompanied by pumping beats. The soundtrack to her new life is mixed by some mythical super DJ. My soundtrack is a single bell, ringing slowly and relentlessly, like my heartbeat. I know I'll be in trouble if it stops. This bell is my expectation and hope.

By the end of the day, we've packed and unpacked a hundred different outfits. My head is spinning. I have to remind myself that this isn't a holiday, a relaxing vacation. I am searching for the one thing that could . . . might explain my life.

That night I can't close my eyes. My body doesn't want to rest, shut down. I go over every minute detail of my life. Friends I've known in nursery school. Friends I've lost in secondary school. I try to remember every birthday party I've had, some by picture only, others by memory. After that I move on to Christmases. All night I try to make sense of my family. I try to mark the time or place when I knew what being part of the Harris family meant. I go through my mental photo album. I study faces. What are the weaknesses we are trying so desperately to hide?

My father is my mother's weakness. She fell in love, instead of making a choice. My father is perpetually on the brink of success; the promotion always round the corner, a few months down the line.

My father's weakness is unfortunately obvious to everyone who knows him. While my mum got on with her life, began to make the tough choices, the ones that made me thankful I'm technically a child, my father stayed safely put in Never Never Land. He is no Peter Pan — he lacks the exuberance that part requires. His eyes are always unfocused, like a mole in daylight. I sometimes wonder what he sees through those lazy blue slits. Does he see my mother's bitterness and disappointment? Is that why he never fully opens his eyes, because he can't bear to see the truth?

As for my small siblings, their eyes are open to all the possibilities that life has. No judgement, no expectations. My parents, caught up in their own confusion, might be blind to

the hate and love I issue in equal doses. But my brother and sisters feel my absence before I've even left. We are connected by the invisible thread of survival.

Naomi

It's exactly three months since Mum started trying to attract her perfect soul mate, and I have a worrying feeling she's starting to lose heart.

Lily tells my mother that she's got to allow for the fact that she's been a cosmic victim for years and years. 'Book or no book, you can't become a spiritual master overnight,' she says calmly. 'Keep radiating positivity and the universe *has* to deliver. It's a cosmic law.'

We're in Lily's kitchen. The windows are all misted over. There's an apple pie in the oven. A pan of home-made vegetable soup simmers gently on the stove. Delicious smells leak under the lid. The room is cosy and steamy but suddenly there's the tiniest chill in the air.

Mum says, 'Well, personally I don't see what's wrong with giving the universe a helping hand.'

And instead of arguing her out of this negative frame

75

of mind, Lily suddenly looks tired and takes a breath. 'You'll just have to do what's right for you,' she says.

We're supposed to stay to supper but Mum suddenly remembers she has to develop some pictures, so we leave hours earlier than planned.

When we get back home, I expect my mother to go up to her studio. But she bangs about in the kitchen defrosting some mince she's had in the freezer for about a year. She starts making a spaghetti sauce, peeling and chopping onions, scowling and muttering to herself.

'I thought we didn't eat meat any more,' I say timidly.

But I don't think Mum's mind is on the task in hand, because she suddenly yells, 'Shit!' Dashing to the sink, she holds her bleeding finger under the cold tap.

I rush to find the medical kit. 'I wonder why you did that?' I say helpfully as I stick on a plaster.

Mum snatches her hand back. 'For Christ's sake!' she snaps. 'Can't a person just cut their sodding finger in this house!'

One evening I catch my mother reading the soul-mates columns. She's circled one of the ads. *Edward*

Rochester, marooned in the Midlands, seeks his Jane.

I'm horrified. I may not be a spiritual master, but I'm fairly sure you can't just terminate a complex cosmic process like Creating Your Own Reality and decide to make your own arrangements.

I smuggle the telephone into my room, carefully feeding the cord under the door.

'Mum's *hopeless*,' I moan to Kumara. 'If I didn't hide her Christmas presents she'd open them by Christmas Eve. I mean, what if the real Mr Right is on his way and she messes it up chasing after some loser who's so desperate, he's advertising himself like a – a second-hand lawn mower?'

'Isn't Rochester the guy in that book who kept his mad wife in his attic?' says Kumara.

'*Jane Eyre*,' I say miserably. 'Thanks for reminding me.'

'Don't worry, Nomes,' Kumara says comfortingly as she hangs up. 'What will be will be.'

One night I come home from the cinema and find a strange man in our kitchen. He's tall, dark and craggily good looking – like Mr Rochester in fact. There's nothing overtly creepy about him. I can't really explain why I get that sudden skin-crawling feeling.

Mum appears in the doorway. She's got an indefinable new shimmer about her. It could be her new eye shadow. More likely it's the prospect of S.E.X. 'Naomi,' she says brightly. 'This is Maurice.'

Carrie-Anne

Matt and I are watching our favourite film *Blade* in my bedroom.

'That guy is pure quality,' Matt says, enthused. 'I never get tired of watching this.'

'Me neither,' I say, trying to snuggle closer.

'Hey, give a guy some personal space.' He rolls off the bed. 'What's with you these days?'

'Nothing,' I lie. I don't have the courage to tell him that ever since I've turned sixteen, I've had this nagging sense that something more should be happening, like Matt and I should somehow take our friendship to the next level.

'Don't go all funny on me, Carrie. I have enough freaked-out women in my life without you joining in.'

'I'm not freaked out. Just chill.'

Matt goes over to the window. 'Can I open this?'

I nod. 'Sure.'

He leans out and takes a deep breath. 'I don't want to have this conversation with you.'

It takes me a while to form the words, form a reply. The emptiness my silence leaves makes me dizzy. I know what is coming. I know what he will say. But it's like when you drive by a car wreck, and you can't stop yourself from looking.

'Then don't.' I wish my voice sounded confident and clear, less like the frightened little girl I am.

He sits down again. 'You're looking for something that isn't there. All this stuff with your mum has just got you stressed out. And we'll sort it out . . . believe me, we will. But don't—' He stops.

'What?'

'I like you a lot, Carrie. You're like a sister. But I don't love you like that and I don't want to sleep with you. It would just mess everything up.'

All I can do is giggle nervously as I feel my heart breaking. 'You've got it all wrong. Mum's just doing my head in, that's all.'

'But you still want to take this trip?' His voice loses its edge and he is back to the old Matt.

'Yeah . . . I think. I just wish Mum would lay off me.'

'You're too similar, you and your mum, that's your problem. You both have that same crazy laugh. Like a dirty old man who smokes too many fags. And when you're thinking you stick your tongues out like village idiots.'

'Thanks! You're just brimming with goodwill tonight. Why are you being so harsh all of a sudden?'

Matt moves over to the window again and lights a cigarette. 'I'm not being harsh. It's just . . . remember your tenth birthday? You spent the entire year going on about that Barbie Dream House. That ugly yellow plastic crap. Man, morning, noon and night you obsessed about that thing. Then the day before your birthday, when your father had become tired of your whining, he suggested that they'd bought you your dream present, and what did you do?'

'I know what I did. I'm not stupid — I was there, remember.'

'You decided right there and then that you'd changed your mind. You wanted a Ballerina Barbie instead. It's the same old same old with you. You always change your mind at the last minute and sprint as far away from your dream as is humanly possible.'

'You think that's what I'm doing? Running away? Maybe

what I want isn't what I thought I wanted. Do you think that—?'

He throws his cigarette butt out of the window. 'Don't ask me to make this decision for you. Can't and won't do it. You decide and we'll try to follow.'

Matt's analysis of my birthday is rather more complex than the truth I remember. I'd only wanted the Dream House because it was the most expensive toy I could find; I'd dreamed about the Ballerina Barbie all along. I guess part of me was just testing my parents' love, pushing to see how much I was worth to them. I hadn't really expected them to be so giving, to actually grant me my one wish. The un-expected always caught me off guard, still does.

Naomi

Mum is singing Maurice Skinner's praises to Lily in our kitchen. 'It's utter bliss. He's everything I need. Intelligent, sexy, *solvent*!'

Lily sounds tentative. 'Do you love him though?'

'I can't believe that woman sometimes,' Mum says when Lily goes home. 'She's supposed to be my best friend but she's actually jealous.'

I'd love to share Mum's belief that Maurice the librarian is the soul mate she's had on order since the dawn of time. It's true that he does all the right soul-mate things. Surprising her with flowers. Cooking intimate little dinners for two.

Yet each time he appears I feel like I did just before a storm when I was little: queasy and breathless, as if Maurice is somehow using up all my oxygen.

My symptoms grow so severe, I have to get a new

inhaler, even though I haven't needed one for years.

Two nights later, Mum and Maurice have their first quarrel.

I cuddle Dizzy in the dark, trying not to hear the raised voices: Mum sounds on the verge of hysteria; Maurice is bored and reasonable.

The fight goes on and on like a storm which never ever breaks.

At last the front door slams and I hear Maurice's footsteps hurrying down the street to his car.

Mum bursts into my room. 'How can he walk away like that!' she weeps. 'I was pouring out my heart, Naomi. I was trying to talk about our *relationship*, and that unfeeling bastard just went on watching the *news*.'

Next day I overhear her cooing to the unfeeling bastard on the phone. 'You should have said your allergies were bothering you. Did I tell you Naomi's asthma started up again? Yes, she must have developed a sensitivity to cat hairs too.'

I run out of the bathroom clutching my towel. 'I haven't!' I plead. 'I could never ever be allergic to Dizzy.'

Mum's eyes narrow. 'First, you have no right to listen

to my private phone calls, Naomi. Second, if you're not allergic to the cat, what the *hell* is causing your *sodding* asthma?'

We stare at each other. It's like a rerun of all the times she threw me over when I was little. I've never ever shouted at my mother before, but I shout at her now. 'You're NOT having him put to sleep!' I scream. 'He's going to the Cats Protection League and I'll take him there MYSELF!' And I run out, weeping.

Poor innocent Dizzy isn't the last living creature to be sacrificed on the altar of Mum and Maurice's relationship.

One morning Lily appears on the doorstep.

I fling my arms around her. 'We haven't seen you for ages! Where's Kumara and Ruby? Did they stop off at the shop?'

'No, sorry, angel. They're at home. I wanted a quick word with Allie.' Lily seems unusually subdued.

My mother is clearly not pleased to see her. 'Say what you've got to say,' she says coldly. 'But I warn you, it won't make any difference.'

She shoos me up to my room but I only pretend to go. I actually sit on the stairs, so I hear everything through the closed door. Lily has been talking to an ex of Maurice's, and what she heard really disturbed her. This woman said that Maurice was a strange fish, cold, controlling.

Lily sounds genuinely worried. 'Naomi's had to put up with a lot of changes in her life, Allie. If you want my advice, you need to think long and hard about what you're getting into—'

I hear Mum marching to the front door before Lily even finishes her sentence. 'I don't want your advice,' she yells. 'And *no one* comes between me and Naomi. Now get out!'

I wait for Lily to say that this is a chance for their friendship to grow deeper and stronger. She and Mum can turn this negative experience into a positive, but she just leaves. She doesn't even say goodbye.

I go up to my room like a zombie. I can't exactly describe how I feel, but it's like an essential piece of machinery has broken inside my chest. I slept over at the Macsweenys' so many times, I kept a spare nightie there.

Ruby and Kumara had shared my hairbrush so often that our three hair types got all tangled up together in the bristles. By this time it was impossible to tell where theirs ended and mine began.

I shut my bedroom door, walk over to my notice board and unpin the photo-booth snaps of Kumara, Ruby and me pulling mad faces in our Wonder Girl costumes. If I leave them up, Mum will rip them down for me.

I unfasten my ancient friendship bracelet, put it inside an envelope with the photos and hide it under my mattress. I wish I could take down the star map which Kumara patiently helped me copy onto my ceiling. I just pray that Mum doesn't notice and insist on painting it out.

That night I lie awake for hours with a draughty space against my ribs where a purring Dizzy ought to be.

I'm not crying, I'm not actually feeling that much. I just lie there staring at my endangered starscape, and I make myself a promise. I say, 'One day, Naomi, you're going to leave.'

Mum's on-off relationship with Maurice drags into

months, then years. And I discover a new skill. I can switch off.

I set off to school, leaving my mother in a puddle of tears because of something Maurice did or didn't do. I get on the bus, take a book out of my school bag and *whoosh!* like the Wonder Girls, I'm bullet-proof.

I see my reflection in the window, calm face, shiny hair. I almost scare myself I'm functioning so well: getting As and Bs in all my subjects, going out with friends – well, not friends exactly, but companions of my own age.

'Don't you care what I'm going through?' Mum rages. 'Haven't you got a heart? Haven't you got *feelings?*'

Is she kidding? Why would anyone want to have feelings? I don't want to care about anyone or anything ever again. It hurts too much.

Carrie-Anne

The sound of Matt's horn makes my mother shudder and leave the hall. I follow her into the kitchen. She is rummaging frantically through her handbag, her back turned towards me. What her face is saying, I don't know. What she feels is even more of a mystery. Without turning she thrusts out a clenched fist, bulging with ten-pound notes.

'I don't want you starving. You're far too skinny as you are. I don't want *her* thinking I haven't been feeding you properly all these years.'

I wish I could tell her to stick it up her arse. I wish I could tell her to go to hell. But I can't. I won't. I need the money. Carl and Gemma are always broke. And Matt? Well, he misplaces his wallet frequently. I am like their personal walking and talking money machine.

Far off I hear Matt's horn again. It has been half an hour and I still can't find Jelly Bean.

'Mum, could you say bye to Jelly Bean for me? I don't think she's going to show.'

'Poor thing's been a wreck since your little drama began. I wish you'd thought more about her. She's only a baby.'

If my mum could crush me any more, I'd be turned inside out. Poke poke. Prod prod.

'Well that's what I'm like. Isn't that right, Mum? If I was really one of you, more like you, I'd know my place, right?'

Her body stiffens. She drops the money and walks through the French doors into the garden. I look down at the pretty pieces of paper lying on the floor, decide that this is one money machine that is now out of order and leave.

We cruise down the motorway at ninety miles per hour, a flash of silver and walnut dashboard. Soft air hisses out of the cooling system, making my skin prickle. The car is so smooth, I feel like I'm gliding on ice. Matt swerves aggressively in and out of the cars, playing an imaginary game of cat and mouse with the other drivers. We begin to slow down and I see a neverending line of cars ahead. Tyres screech, horns honk. The universal signal for a traffic jam. One hour on the road and we're already queuing impatiently. We're like sardines wedged into a tin too small to accommodate our salty, sweaty bodies.

Gem is sitting up front, one bare foot with angry red painted toenails hanging out of the window. Carl is snoring like a beast beside me. His hands seem weirdly alive, electric currents running through them: even in sleep he is magnetic. I've always been pulled by Carl's gravitational field. Maybe it's because he possesses the gentlest, most breathtaking smile, a smile that even Matt can't compete with. He's been spinning discs at the Buddha Bar until sunrise. When he is asleep, he looks like the child he is. I sometimes forget Carl's only seventeen. He has seen things, been to places I could never imagine. His mother, Bella, took him to India when he was six; they travelled around for years. No teeth brushing, no rough flannel behind the ears, just sweet saffron and smoked paprika. Bella comes and goes now. They're more like students sharing a crappy flat than mother and son, their lives constantly criss-crossing, never really touching. While my mother's idea of a hobby is stencilling wild-flower designs on wooden picture frames, Carl's mother is the woman next to the bar in the club, handing out the pills and the condoms.

Gem turns in her seat and gives me a wicked grin. 'Shall we shave off his eyebrows? Or what about a makeover? Blue eye shadow? Pink cheeks? He won't notice, you know. Once he's asleep the outbreak of a third world war wouldn't wake him. Come on, Carrie-Anne, let's be naughty.'

'I think you're naughty enough all on your own, you bad girl. Leave your little man to his peace.'

Gem sticks out her lower lip. 'I hope you're going to be more fun than this when we get to Cornwall.'

I look out of the window at the other cars and wonder if we are all going to the same place. If we are all queuing for the same thing. I decide Gemma could be right. Life would be so much easier if we were all stand-up comedians. Everything ironic, everything observational, all the pain in someone else's back yard.

The Smokers' Club congregate by the side of the road. I huddle in the back of the car. I feel excluded from their intimate group. The secrets they share over cigarettes are unknown to me. I don't belong with them in that moment, when they inhale and exhale.

They stand, my friends, paper cutouts against the wonder

of the setting sun. A Jackson Pollock of spewed pink and fiery orange. I realize I can't remember the last time I actually looked up at the sky to simply enjoy its abstract canvas of soft white, pale blue and dove-grey. Lately I haven't taken time to look at anything properly.

My friends flick their cigarette butts into the road. Red sparks fly at the oncoming cars. The car is suddenly full of hot bodies and the stale smell of nicotine.

'You all right?' Gem tugs at my ponytail. 'We're hungry – you want to join us for some really crap service station food?'

I nod, only half listening.

'Daydreamer! What's on your mind?'

Matt turns in the driver's seat, his shades low on his nose, giving him the impression of a strict librarian. Carl is frantically fiddling with the radio. The rush of static and garbled snatches of sound gives me a headache. He snaps it off and slumps back, defeated.

'Are there no good tunes on the radio? Did you guys bring some mini discs? Not you, Gem. I'm sick of listening to euro dance crap!'

Matt and I look at each other blankly. Carl's only tangible role in life is King of the Decks. The beat master, whose

drum is loyally followed by us, his devoted teenage fan club. Pump pump. We gyrate, we twist, we turn and leap, following our Technics Pied Piper towards the strobing lights.

Matt looks worried. 'What, no sounds? You, mate, are without tunes?'

Even Gemma has gone quiet. She leans over and softly touches Carl's forehead. 'Are you all right?'

He flinches away as though her hand emits static shocks. 'I fluffed.'

Matt switches off the engine. The silence it leaves behind is uncomfortable. Carl didn't fluff. We all know that. We all depend on that fact.

'What do you mean?' Gem's voice is barely audible over the whoosh of passing cars. Her eyes are wide, like a deer in the headlights of a truck.

Carl begins to pick at the leather seat, deliberately avoiding all eye contact. He takes a deep breath and begins.

'The Buddha Bar was important for me. You guys just don't get it. You never have. You think this is all I'm about. We all know Carrie-Anne has a first-class ticket straight to

Oxford or some smart university. Matt, mate . . . well, we all know you're going to get by. And Gem . . .' He looks down at his hands. 'Gem will no doubt get a nice cushy secretarial job at her dad's firm.'

He settles back in his seat and looks out of the window again. 'The Buddha Bar was my ticket. But I screwed that one up, didn't I? I took the back room. Marcus was up front. The place was heaving. The crowd was feeling it. I felt like a fucking god. My set was peaking and . . . my vinyl wasn't in order. I'd been chilling the day before, got to spinning some tunes and just forgot about the gig. I couldn't get it back. I lost it. I lost it in front of everyone. I've been unplugged. I've decided . . . I've decided that I'm going to stay in Newquay.'

I close my eyes and struggle to concentrate on the rhythm of the traffic passing by.

Naomi

It's only six thirty but the streets are pitch-dark. The scabby little recreation ground near our house is littered with old snow.

This is the first time I've been out for weeks. I'm so weak and wobbly that just the wail of a police car in the next street makes my heartbeat quicken.

In our Macsweeny days, I'd have been dosed with some weird holistic remedy. Lily and Mum would have put their heads together, trying to work out why I'd got ill in the first place. Was it something at school? Had anyone upset me lately?

This time Mum just said I had to stop being such a bloody crybaby and pull myself together. She seemed so certain I was faking my symptoms that I believed her and carried on dragging myself to school. Finally I fainted in assembly and they sent me home. Our doctor made me have a blood test. It turned out I wasn't a cry-baby after all. I had glandular fever.

Mum was so ashamed that she cried and begged me to forgive her.

I've been off school for months. The best thing about my illness is that our house has become a blissfully Maurice-free zone.

'He really cares about you, sweetie. He just can't cope with illness. He's too sensitive,' Mum kept telling me.

Now they must think I'm out of the woods. Maurice rang Mum from work this morning to announce that he was coming round to cook some special middle eastern dish to build up my strength. He gave Mum a list of groceries she had to buy, only she forgot something important.

Maurice only discovered this as his preparations reached a crucial point, oil spluttering, pans coming to the boil.

'Great,' he said. 'You forgot the coriander.'

Maurice believes in self control. He never throws crockery, never raises his voice. But I always know when he's angry because my gut starts to churn.

'They sell coriander at our corner shop,' I told him hastily.

His nostrils flared. 'The Asian shop?' For someone so keen on foreign food Maurice is surprisingly suspicious of other cultures.

'Yeah, the Moral Minimart. Mum and I go there all the time.'

'Well don't let them fob you off with any old rubbish,' he snorted.

The shop is just at the end of our street, but by the time I've walked there and back I'm trembling all over. I've forgotten my door key so I have to totter round to the back of the house.

I catch sight of them together through the window. Mum in her loose white shirt and faded jeans, setting the table, The serious-looking man with greying hair, chopping vegetables at the counter.

The scene makes me ache inside. From here it looks like everything I've ever dreamed of. A mum and dad peacefully preparing food together. Mum's right, I think. I have to stop being so childish. I have to get to know Maurice better, then everything will be all right.

I take a deep breath and go in through the back door, inhaling delicious smells of cinnamon and mint and lemon peel. My chilled muscles instantly relax in the steamy warmth of the kitchen. I hold out the crumpled brown paper bag stuffed with sharply-scented coriander.

'I got the last bunch,' I say proudly. Now maybe Maurice will see how hard I'm trying. That I want to make this work as much as they do.

Maurice smiles his tight little smile. 'It's too late now, Naomi. You took too long.'

He lifts the lid of the pedal bin so I can see all the wasted food steaming inside.

One Saturday I bump into Kumara in town. I've seen her before loads of times. We've even exchanged a few stilted greetings. But until today some invisible force field seemed to be keeping us apart. Now, miraculously, it's gone. We hug other, laughing and crying.

Kumara's friends don't seem to know what to make of our damp and blubbery reunion. They're all dressed identically: tiny black skirts, skimpy black tops and Doc

Martens. Suddenly I feel like the good wholesome girl in *Grease*.

Kumara tells her friends to go on without her. She takes me into The Oasis, our local wholefood café, and stumps up for coffee and huge apricot flapjacks.

Things are creaky at first. We were barely thirteen when our mothers stopped talking. Now we're both studying for O levels. But soon we're chatting away like old times.

'Do you still want to go to drama school?' I ask her.

Kumara flicks back her hair. 'Definitely. I've just started going to the local youth theatre group. It's brilliant fun. You should come.'

I duck my head. 'I don't know. I think maybe I'm one of life's watchers.'

'What a load of crap,' she says affectionately.

We munch away at our industrial-sized flapjacks, then Kumara says, 'Hey, did you hear Mum's studying to be a lawyer?'

'No way! Do they let lawyers wear nose studs now?'

'Ah, but there *is* no stud,' she grins. 'No shalwar kameez either. Mum's depressingly conventional these days.'

'Seriously?'

Kumara laughs. 'Only on the outside. She's still as mad as a hatter inside.'

Inevitably we get round to Maurice.

'I hate him.' My voice shakes.

Kumara touches my hand. 'He hasn't, you know, *hurt* you?'

I can't explain that what Maurice does is almost worse. How he fills a room with killer vibes just by walking in. How he uses up all the available oxygen so I have to fight him just for the right to breathe. How it's no use me even holding an opinion, because he makes everything I say seem like the ignorant babblings of a silly little girl.

'Mum says I don't even make an effort to like him, but she has no idea. I try so hard my eyes water.'

'If he treats her so badly, why does she want you to like him?' says Kumara, puzzled.

I pull a face. 'It's complicated.'

'She wants to cry on your shoulder when it suits her, then when it's all lovey-dovey, you're meant to shower them with confetti, is that it?'

'Kind of,' I admit. 'She thinks he's her last shot at

living happily ever after. She's going to make him into Mr Right if it kills her.' I start to explain how, at the age of thirty-six, Mum is convinced she already has one foot in the grave, but Kumara interrupts.

'Talking of Mr Right,' she says mischievously, 'did you notice that boy in the corner? No, don't turn round, he'll see.'

'Who are we talking about exactly?' I say.

'Adam Hayden. He goes to the same school as my friend Lucy's brother. He's a genius – a total weirdo but a genius. He's been staring at you ever since we came in.'

'Don't be stupid.' I can feel myself going bright red.

Kumara's eyes flicker slyly to the group of boys in the corner then back. 'Oh, Naomi,' she breathes. 'He's drawing something on a napkin. I think he's drawing *you*!'

'Shut up,' I hiss back. 'Anyway, I don't believe you.'

The back of my neck feels rigid from the effort of not looking round. And I'd swear under oath that I never actually *do* turn round at any point.

So how is it that when I get home, I have a flawless mental photograph of the dark-haired, dark-eyed genius weirdo in the corner?

That night, as I check through my history essay, I notice I've been scribbling on the inside of the exercise book. The same word over and over. Adam Adam Adam Adam . . .

It's his hands I remember, square with stubby fingers, yet electric with energy. And his hair, jet-black like blackbird's feathers.

Is it possible to absorb that kind of information through your skin? Is it possible that I might have a functioning heart after all?

Carrie-Anne

After Carl's little bombshell, none of us really feels much like eating. I begin to get that icky feeling in my tummy, the one that says, 'I told you to trust your instincts, and you just couldn't be bothered.' I should have flown this mission solo. I have enough emotional baggage for all my friends put together. I'd forgotten they all carried their own jumbo-sized holdalls of pain and grief. I feel trapped. Gem, Matt and Carl are suddenly strangers. Passers-by I've got stuck on the train with. People I don't want to know. I can feel the conflict growing in my stomach, biley confusion reaching up into my throat. Is it too late to turn round and pretend none of this is real, that none of it has actually happened? Can I turn and look at my family, my friends and remember why I love them? I've felt lonely before. But the agony of feeling that there isn't a single person in existence who under-stands the ache inside is new and terrifying.

All the en-route dramas have set our journey back an hour. We don't arrive in Newquay until the evening. By this time the battle of the sexes has begun. I'm not sure who starts it. I guess it's natural. Matt and Carl are sitting up front together and it's like one of those 'girls v. boys' scenarios as we try to find a campsite. Matt and Carl just can't admit they don't have a sense of direction. They are completely opposed to the idea that we know more about navigation then they do. Eventually, after a hundred and one wrong turns, we reach our destination. A place called Lonely Farm – a ramshackle house surrounded by ruins of farm buildings. The drive up to the farm is two miles at least. The nearest inhabitants are even further away. At Lonely Farm, truly, no one would hear you scream. The site manager is a hairy dwarf of a man called Jed. He takes us to the so-called campsite, which is in actual fact a muddy field, cordoned off with barbed-wire fencing. There are a couple of wooden sheds that have been haphazardly assembled to make a toilet and shower room. It looks more like a concentration camp than a holiday destination.

'What's this?' Gem asks, waving a tent peg in my face.

'Don't be such a girl! And don't pretend like you don't

know,' Carl says tersely. 'I know you were a girl guide.'

'Was not!' Gem exclaims, looking at me accusingly. 'I can't believe you told him that,' she mouths at me.

I shrug. 'Oh, come on, Gem. You were well into that whole collecting badges thing!'

'Great, then let's have a little competition,' Matt says, rubbing his hands together. 'Girls versus boys, loser cooks dinner.'

'Oh, what fun!' I sound like a whiny five-year-old, but I'd expected this whole trip to be like something from one of those soppy American road-trip movies, not an instalment of *Blue Peter*. 'And then we can sit around the campfire and tell ghost stories. Fun, fun, fun!'

'I'm with Carrie,' Gem chimes in. 'This whole thing is super shit. It's cold; therefore these lily-white legs are going to get no sun action. And my trainers are totally covered in mud – and what is that smell? It makes me want to puke! I have a much better idea. Why don't you boys put up both tents while Carrie and I sit in the car?'

Gem's exit would have been incredibly stylish if she hadn't then slipped and landed face down in the muddy field. I haven't laughed so hard for months, maybe years. A balloon of anxiety has been building in my body and Gem's unintended act of slapstick is the pin that releases the tension. I laugh and it feels real. I know my duties as best friend should involve me tenderly helping her to her feet and shooting dirty looks at Carl and Matt.

'Um, I'll go and put up the girls' tent. Carrie, why don't you help Gem get, um, cleaned up?' Carl splutters.

Matt is too weak from hysterics to do anything but nod, tears streaming down his face. I go to help Gem to her feet but she sharply pulls away.

'I can manage on my own, thank you very much. Why don't you go and help Carl?'

Later that evening, as we struggle into our sleeping bags, the image of Gem's unfortunate encounter with the mud is still haunting me and I can't help chuckling away to myself.

'It wasn't that funny. Besides, you should have taken my side. You always have to show off in front of Carl and Matt. Be one of the lads. It makes me sick.'

I'm startled. 'What do you mean? I don't show off.'

'Yeah right! Everyone knows you do. We all talk about it.'

'We? What we?'

'Holly, Carmen, Kate, Pretty – everyone.'

I can't believe what I'm hearing. 'Just because you're pissed off about things being sticky between you and Carl there's no need to download your poo onto me. It's not my fault you guys can't stop arguing.'

'That's not why I brought it up. I've been meaning to mention something about this for ages.'

'Great timing!'

Gem twists and turns in her sleeping bag. 'It's beginning to do my nut, that's all. Oh, and there's something else I've been meaning to tell you.'

I don't like her tone. I know it. I've seen her use it on other victims. I always try to pretend this side of Gem isn't real. She has a gift for knowing exactly what will hurt, and when it will cause most pain. 'Well, I really don't want to know right now. I have enough on my plate without your silly little games. Can we just leave this and go to sleep?'

'I'm not playing games, Carrie-Anne. I just thought you'd like to know about what happened after Chaos . . . that's all.'

I'm glad for darkness in the tent, I'm glad I can't see her expression and she can't see my hurt. 'Oh, for God's sake tell me then. What happened that was so special after Chaos?'

'I didn't say it was special, but I thought you should know. Matt and I had sex.'

It's like being punched in the stomach. I can't breathe. 'What?'

I know Gem is rolling her eyes. 'It's not a big deal. It was just shagging.'

'Why you and not me?'

'Does that matter?' Gem zips her sleeping bag and plumps up her pillow. 'It was just one of those things. We were high on all the atmosphere—'

'And other things,' I butt in. 'How could you do this to me?'

'I didn't. We did. And it's all done and dusted now. We got it out of our systems.'

'Maybe I need more than five seconds to recover from my best friend – or should I say, the person I thought was my best friend – betraying me.' I'm trying hard not to cry. I don't want her to see that she's successfully driven a stake through my heart.

'This is what I was talking about. Maybe Matt came to me because I'm more relaxed. You make everything so serious, so about you. Now can I please get some sleep? I'm knackered.'

I close my eyes and repeat my secret mantra in my head: 'I don't care. I don't care. I don't care.' I discovered years ago that if I said it enough, I'd feel a numbness overcoming me. A kind of anaesthetic for my soul. I'm still hurting somewhere inside, but can't quite reach it, can't quite feel it. I try to hear something, anything outside, so I know I haven't gone deaf. My dad told me once that in films when there is a silence, they play something called 'room tone'. I didn't understand what this meant until tonight. I never realized that silence has a sound. If you listen hard enough, long enough, you can hear the grass growing, the birds shifting in their nests and even the clouds moving across the sky. The silence is so deep you can feel it reverberate through your skin, bones and blood.

Naomi

Since I've been revising for exams I've noticed a strange phenomenon. No sooner do I look up a new word in the dictionary than it starts coming at me from all directions – TV, radio, the daily newspaper; that word is suddenly everywhere, yet previously it might as well not have existed.

It's like that with Adam. We've lived in the same claustrophobic little town our whole lives and I'd never once set eyes on him. Now, like a new addition to my vocabulary, he's everywhere: at The Oasis, in the cinema, at the next table in the local library.

I could almost believe some cosmic power was deliberately throwing us together.

That's just stupid; what Maurice calls 'magical thinking'. Stuff happens, that's all. Knives slip. People meet and get asthma. Only to primitive tribes and sad old hippies do these events have to make sense. That's what

I tell myself at least. But then I think of Adam, and my grim 'life is meaningless' scenario falls apart.

What I'm feeling is so intense, so strange, so beautiful, it *has* to be love.

The instant he appears, even if I don't see him come in, I feel it inside, as if we're connected by an invisible thread.

When he's not around, I can't stop thinking of him. I want to say his name constantly.

One time I creep out of the house in my dressing gown and call Kumara from a phone box. I'm hopping from foot to foot, teeth rattling with cold, desperately trying to think up some lame excuse to bring him into the conversation.

As it turns out, Kumara brings him up herself.

Her friend Lucy is going out with Adam's older brother. 'The whole Hayden family is nuts, if you ask me,' Kumara says. 'Their parents have an open marriage, hopping into bed with anyone they fancy. Have you ever heard of anything so disgusting?'

I'm righteous on Adam's behalf. 'I don't see how that could possibly work!'

'Of course it couldn't. Last year their dad fell for this younger woman. He moved out, but the younger woman got sick of him, so he moved back in again. Can you imagine the vibes?'

I shake my head.

'Now his mum and dad are either yelling their heads off, or ignoring each other and just leaving messages on the fridge. Lucy says it hit Adam really hard. He stopped going to school, literally didn't leave the house for weeks. They had to send him to a counsellor. He's back in the sixth form now, but if he doesn't like the teacher, he just walks out. I told you, Naomi, he's weird.'

I'm staring at a cigarette end someone's trodden into the floor. Kumara is still talking, but I've stopped listening. Three words are circling inside my head like hopeful birds.

Adam needs me.

Mum comes into my room after I've put my light out. She probably figures my defences will be down in the dark. Her voice is syrupy with concern. She says, 'Sweetie, I'm worried about you. You're changing.'

I hunch irritably under the covers. 'Meaning?'

'Meaning I hardly know you any more.'

'Oh, so what's changed exactly?' I say coldly.

Mum swallows. 'I just hope you'd tell me if there was ever a problem.'

'Oh, yeah?' I say. '*Then* what would you do?'

I want to laugh out loud. I want to slap her face. But mostly I just want her to get out of my room so I can go back to thinking about Adam.

I saw him two days ago at The Oasis with his friends. That is, he was sitting at their table, but you could see he wasn't really part of their group, just as I wasn't really part of mine.

'I know I haven't exactly . . .' Mum is saying.

I shut my eyes to make her go away, so I can imagine how it'll be when we're finally alone together.

In these blissful fantasies, there's never any need to talk or explain. Just being together feels so right. When we kiss, we'll flow together like spilled mercury. It'll be like finding the last piece of the puzzle.

Like coming home.

Carrie-Anne

Next morning my body and brain refuse to wake up. My sleeping bag feels safe; it smells like home, like my childhood. I keep my eyes tight shut and can almost believe I'm six years old again. I'd forgotten that I wasn't always this cynical, so disappointed, so like my mother. I can feel Gem moving restlessly about in her sleeping bag beside me. The air has become stale with sleep. It makes me feel queasy. I've spent most of the night trying to figure out what to do and say to Matt and Gemma. My life experience feels so small and insignificant suddenly. I don't know what you do when your friends betray you. I know I want to lash out, draw blood, make them feel my pain.

'I'm going to make some coffee. You want some?'

All I get in response is a grunt, followed by a thumbs up. Outside, the sun is already attempting to make a star appearance through the mass of clouds. The morning dew

glints like a multitude of diamonds all over the grass. Everything is still. The only sound is the croaky cry of the cockerel and the conversational tweeting of the dawn birds. Carl is crouched over the camping stove, busy boiling a pan of water.

'Great minds think alike, I see.' I yawn, settling myself down on the damp grass beside him. 'Was going to make some coffee myself. You're up early.'

'Yeah, well, who can sleep when Matt's snoring away like a beast? The sounds that come out of that guy's nostrils are deafening. Think I eventually passed out from exhaustion at around four a.m.'

'Poor you.'

'One lump or two?'

'Three — need some zap to get me going. I didn't get much sleep last night either.'

Carl hands me a mug of steaming coffee. 'Worrying about your mum?'

I don't have the heart to tell Carl the truth, not yet anyway. Matt never made me any promises, he was my mate. Gemma was Carl's girlfriend, which puts his betrayal in a whole different league to mine. 'Something like that. Had some really odd dreams though.'

'Me too. I had this dream – more of a nightmare – that I was in this bar trying to get it on with a group of these really hot FHM babes, and all that would come out of my mouth were these cheesy chat-up lines, like "Did it hurt when you fell from heaven?" Nearly woke up screaming.'

'Again, poor you.'

'What did you dream about?'

'Stuff. I only remember bits and bobs. I know Mum and Dad were in it somewhere. But it was more the feelings that unnerved me. I don't know.' I pause and look at the sky, look anywhere but at Carl. 'I feel like I'm making a huge mistake being here.'

'I thought you wanted to meet Naomi?'

'Yeah, I do. I'm worried about my other mum. I think I went overboard with this whole trip ... took it too far. I treated Mum like shit.'

Carl throws the dregs of the coffee over his shoulder and begins to roll a cigarette. 'It's what us teenagers do. Why the sudden change of heart?'

'This morning when I woke up ... it reminded me of

being little again. You know, feeling safe and sure. I feel like a total fuck-up.'

'We're all one of those.' Carl lights his cigarette. 'You know what, though? Your mum's always been good to us. She didn't bat an eyelid when Matt got banged up for six months or when Gem had one of her regular spaz outs. I'd say she was pretty level headed.'

'Yeah, she's a saint with everyone else, just not me.'

'At least she's there and she cares.'

'She's there, but whether she cares is a whole other issue. She didn't even say goodbye to me.'

'Doesn't mean there's no love. I've had about three conversations with Bella in the past seven months. Admittedly it's because she's never there, but I still know that in her funny, drugged-up way she still cares. You just have to look deep . . . really, really deep.' Carl begins to get up. 'Anyway, the call of nature has struck.'

I smile up at him. 'Think I'll take a wander before the other two finally emerge from their sleeping bags.'

I watch as Carl jogs off towards the makeshift toilets. The mobile phone in my pocket suddenly starts to beep and vibrate. I nearly drop it with shock when I see there's a text message from my mum. She thinks texting is the tool of the devil, that children will soon begin to talk in text speak and lose any grasp they once had over the English language. 'Good morning, Carrie. Remember to brush your teeth.' That's all it says.

I struggle through rough grasses and spiky heather, past gorse bushes that surprisingly reek of coconut suntan lotion, until I come to the sea.

The beach is actually about a half-mile drop down from the edge of the cliff I am perched on. I can barely breathe. I feel like it is the first dawn sky I've ever seen. The first time I've smelled the pungent sea salt. It forces its way up into my sinuses, plummeting into my lungs, expanding my chest until I'm afraid I'll burst into a million grains of glistening salt, dissolving into the sea.

I can't stop myself. All the anger I feel for Matt and Gemma had been boiling in my stomach and has begun to rise like bile to the back of my throat. My coffee mug goes flying over the cliff and I begin to scream. The sound coming out of me sounds sub-human. I can't help myself, I wail until I am empty. Until all my anger has evaporated into the sea air. And all I want to do is speak to my mother. Not the

fictional one I carry as a weapon to disarm my real mum. I want the woman who held me as I vomited up my baby hurt, my distress. The woman I took my first steps towards, reached out for. The relief I feel at remembering why I love her so much makes salty water run from my eyes. Whatever happens, wherever I go, I know that my point of return will be fixed for ever.

Naomi

'Oh, God, Judd Nelson!' says Kumara.

I'm in my favourite phone box in broad daylight, inhaling stale phone-box smells, twisting the telephone cord around my fingers, listening to Kumara rave about the video of *The Breakfast Club*.

'It sounds great,' I say half-heartedly.

'Come round and watch it with me,' she offers. 'We'll have a Brat Pack orgy. *Pretty in Pink. Sixteen Candles.*'

'I can't. Mum would kill me if she knew I was even talking to you.'

'So don't tell her. You needn't worry about *my* mum. She adores you. She was really worried about you after they had that row. She said she had a good mind to kidnap you and bring you up herself.'

I feel myself going hot with embarrassment. 'Mum's heart is in the right place,' I say defensively. 'She's just

121

going through a bad patch. She and Maurice have split up. For good this time.'

'You don't believe her, do you?' says Kumara scornfully.

I'm not sure I'm a hundred per cent over my glandular fever, because suddenly I have to lean my forehead against the smeary glass.

'I do believe her actually,' I say. 'She met Maurice when she was feeling really vulnerable, but she's finally seen through him. But they've been going out together for three years, so naturally she's upset. Also we've got to move house again, which adds to the stress.'

Kumara sounds horrified. 'She's making you move in the middle of your O levels!'

'It's not Mum's fault,' I say quickly. 'The landlord put the rent up. But it's OK, she's found a flat. And she's not taking our old phone number, so creepy Maurice won't know where we've gone.'

Mum and I have moved so often we could practically do it in our sleep. Wrapping crockery in newspaper, taking down pictures, packing books in Walkers crisp boxes, systematically stripping rooms of all the objects that make them home, and starting again somewhere new.

This latest move frightens Mum, I can tell.

She looks bewildered, almost like a little girl. And I can tell what she's thinking. She's thinking, This is how it's going to be from now on, slipping slowly downhill; each place smaller and more depressing than the last, until finally she's a lonely old lady watching soaps in a poky bedsit.

I'm sorry for her. But I'm careful to keep my distance. I'm not a total sucker, whatever Kumara thinks. Besides, she hasn't seen my mother for ages. She doesn't know how much she's changed. For three years she's been under an evil Maurice spell, but it's wearing off. Some day soon she'll be her true self again.

Last time, we had two adults and three children to help. This time, we just rent a man with a van. Both are nerve-rackingly decrepit. The guy has some kind of heart condition. Twice he goes completely white and has to sit down. We end up shifting the heavy stuff ourselves. By the time he goes it's almost dark.

We watch anxiously, as he drives off in the empty van, rattling and bouncing down the street.

'Hope the poor bastard makes it back home,' Mum mutters. She's so exhausted she can hardly speak.

Our eyes meet and we both burst out laughing for the first time in months. Then suddenly Mum goes all weepy. 'Oh Naomi, you've been so wonderful. I couldn't have coped with this alone.'

She tries to hug me. I stiffen instinctively and she lets me go.

'I don't blame you for being angry,' she says. 'I let that man poison everything between us. I know it's going to take time for you to forgive me. But I can wait, OK? I can wait.'

I search her face in the twilight. There are real tears tracking down her cheeks. 'OK,' I say huskily.

When we go indoors, we discover that the last tenant has taken all the lampshades. Mum and I can't bear the glare of the naked bulbs, so I hunt for the box with the kitchen candles while Mum phones up to order pizza. We picnic by candlelight among the boxes.

We're too tired to assemble our beds, so we make up

mattresses with duvets and pillows and undress in the flickery candle-glow.

Mum calls to me from her mattress across the landing. 'I've got an idea for a new exhibition. "Mothers and Daughters". What do you think?'

Later her drowsy voice floats into my room. 'We'll paint your room first. We'll do it any colour you like. It'll be a new start, sweetie. Just you and me. Like it used to be.'

Carrie-Anne

I wander back to the campsite feeling renewed. For the briefest moment I've moved beyond my pain and confusion and dispelled my dark cloud. I stroll over to our tents feeling more alive than I have for months. I feel like I've been woken from a catatonic state. I've been walking, I've been talking all these months, maybe years, but never really seen or heard anything.

My friends look less animated. Gem is sitting by herself, picking blades of grass. The monotony of her actions begins to diminish my high. She looks dull, like the earth has been one big colouring book for God, and he's forgotten to colour Gem in, all gradations of grey, monochrome and life-less. Matt and Carl don't seem any more active.

Carl is playing with his cigarette lighter, flicking it on and off, twiddling his fingers in the flame. Matt is plugged into his mini-disc player, his foot twitching along to the music. I always like to try and guess what he's listening to, using the silent beat to guide me. Judging by the pace of his jiggling trainer, I'd say it was hip-hop. Matt says hip-hop is raw, rough and tough. The lyrics pound you like a good beating, leaving you bruised, but wiser. I wish the years of listening to it had left him wiser. Then he'd have chosen me and not Gem. Why didn't he choose me? Once again, someone who was supposed to love me has abandoned me. I look to Gem and then to Matt and try not to imagine them together … having sex. I shudder. I used to play this game when I was little: I'd tear pictures of pop stars and Hollywood actors out of magazines and place them alongside a photograph of me, trying to find an exact match. Searching for a possible soul mate. Now I'm standing looking at my two best friends, trying to see if they are a match.

'What's up with you guys?' I say.

'Look around,' Gem says, pulling a face. 'We're in mud hell. And what is the rank smell? Is that you, Carl?'

'No, it's the pig farm, sweet stuff. Didn't you hear them being loaded onto the trucks this morning? Man, I'm never touching bacon again.'

'Is that what all that screaming was? I thought it was Carrie-Anne and Gem,' Matt says lazily.

'I'm so bored. We can't sit around in this field waiting for something to happen.' Gem jumps up. 'Can we please go and look at the sea, so I feel like we're at least *trying* to have fun?'

I stand on the beach by my so-called best friend. She's slapping me on the backside with a rolled-up copy of *Mixmag*.

'Come on! You have to do this. Make the call.'

This isn't just any call we are discussing. It is *the* call. The call that will change my life. In my sweaty hand I hold the dirty piece of paper, ripped out of my diary. It has a flowery background. The image has been faded almost to invisibility by time – I think they're poppies or maybe roses.

'God, Carrie-Anne! You can stand here all day, but it's not going to make it any easier. The best thing is to just get it over with.'

'Gem, I will make the call, but I don't need you being a bloody cheerleader. I need time.'

I know she is rolling her eyes.

'Whatever.'

I hear her walk back towards the others. I know I told her to leave but doesn't she care enough to stay? To hold onto me now that I'm covered in spikes, when I'm on fire and could scorch the skin off her hands and make her insides boil with pain? Recently I've watched Gemma evolve into someone who never really cares. She's been initiated into the ranks of the cool and the distant. The more I am with her, the more I realize I mustn't get too close, get too truthful.

I look down at my mobile phone and feel emptiness. Why am I doing this? What good will it do? What good is it supposed to do?

I press DIAL.

'Hello.'

I go dizzy and all the colour fades from my scenery.

'Hello?'

'Er, can I speak to Naomi please?'

'Oh, I'm sorry, love. She's working in Milan until the end of the week. Can I take a message?'

My mind has fragmented into a million questions. I'm not sure I actually heard what the woman said. Confused, I stumble on.

'Um, when will she be back – I mean, exactly . . . please?'

'Naomi should be back . . . Hang on, I'll just check her schedule.'

I hear rustling papers in the background. I hear the woman calling out and a man with an accent reply. I hear the sea and try to keep standing.

'Hello. Yes, she'll be back on Friday. Can I take a name and number?'

Without thinking I give her my name and mobile number and instantly want to take it back. I press END CALL and crouch on the ground, my head between my knees, and try to breathe slowly in and out. But my heart won't stop pumping. I can hear it pounding in my ears and feel it in my belly. In two days I'll know. In two days I'll meet her and for that I have no script. And then, like in a film, everything fades to black.

Naomi

My exams are finally over. No more revision. No more stress. And I'm on the sofa in my old nightie watching TV, luxuriating in the feeling of having absolutely nothing to do. Mum comes in and out a few times, and finally I say, 'What?'

She gives me her brightest smile. 'I woke up thinking about your bedroom. I'm thinking Arabian Nights. Lovely gauzy fabrics, terracotta and gold paint. So why don't you get washed and dressed and go out and get us some paint charts?'

'You said your cheque hadn't come,' I object. 'We haven't got enough money to buy paint.'

'I know!' she beams. 'But if you get the charts now, we'll be prepared when the cheque does come. We'll be able to leap into action!'

She's in such a sweet, bubbly mood that I decide to humour her.

'OK, slave driver,' I tease.

And I think, She's finally getting over him.

On the way home, I catch sight of Kumara's friend Lucy through the window of The Oasis. She mimes drinking coffee. I just point at my watch and shake my head. I'm not late for anything. I just find Lucy a bit intimidating. To my alarm she comes outside for a chat. In her black clothes and luscious dark lipstick, she looks like a particularly sexy and kissable vampire,

Lucy jokes about how Kumara goes on about me so much, she's getting jealous. She says I must come over to her place with Kumara some time and hang out. Then she tells me about the big all-night party, the youth theatre kids are holding. 'You've *got* to come,' she says dramatically. 'It's going to be *so* fabulous.'

The last time I went to a party, they had chocolate fingers and balloons. I try out the phrase 'all-night party' to myself inside my head. It sounds thrilling and dangerous.

I picture myself walking back home through the sleeping town at sunrise just as the birds start to twitter their dawn chorus. I picture myself being the kind of girl who has experienced an all-night party.

'Well . . .' I say.

Lucy gives me a sly look. 'Did I mention it's at the Haydens' house?'

I want to crawl away and never speak to another human being ever. It's bad enough knowing Kumara's seen through me, but that she discussed me with her friends . . .

Lucy reaches out unexpectedly to touch my hair. 'It's such a pretty colour,' she says, as if she's consoling me for something. 'You should make more of yourself, you know.' Her eyes light up. 'I could give you a makeover! Say you'll let me! I *adore* doing my girlfriends' makeovers.'

On the way home, I'm practically running. I tell myself I'm stupid to feel hurt. Kumara didn't mean to betray my confidence. Lucy didn't mean to humiliate me. And I'm not, I am *not* going to cry in the street like a baby.

I am desperate to get back to my mum. I need her to put her arms around me and say, 'You're worth ten of those little bitches,' the way she did that time I got bullied in the juniors. I need her to say, 'What has love to do with sodding *make-up*, for Christ's sake?' My mother is the only person who really knows me. The only person I can ever trust.

I let myself into the flat. I'm struggling so hard not to cry, I can't seem to make my voice work. In a pathetic voice I croak, 'Mum?'

I hear her voice coming from the sitting room. Something in her tone stops me from going in. I stay frozen to the spot, scarcely breathing because I know exactly who she's talking to.

'I just couldn't imagine going on living without you,' my mother says softly. She sounds like someone talking in her sleep.

In that moment I see everything so clearly that I go completely cold inside.

I'm scared. I'm genuinely scared of what I might do. I back along the corridor to my bedroom and shut myself in.

I keep seeing her eager little smile as she spun me that paint-chart crap, when all the time she wanted me out of the way, so she could talk to *him*!

How could I be so stupid! Letting myself be used, not once, but again and again and again . . .

I rip up the colour charts in a fury. It's not enough. I want to wreck my whole room, tip over furniture, smash lamps. Then I remember my mother hurling cups at walls and I draw a deep, shuddering breath.

I won't, I won't *ever* be like her.

A few minutes later I stroll into the living room, cool as ice.

Mum quickly sets down the phone, looking flustered. 'Naomi, I didn't hear you come back.'

She's wondering how much I've heard.

I don't even look at her. I just dial Lucy's number and hum to myself while I wait for her to pick up.

'Oh, hi, it's Naomi. When did you say that party was again? Yeah, I'd love to. I thought maybe I'd come over to your place first? Yeah, I'd love for you to help me get ready. Don't be silly! Why would I be offended? OK, see ya!'

I replace the phone and stroll back out, all without looking at Mum.

I feel so powerful I could sing out loud. I've seen the

light. No more staying home feeling sorry for my mother. No more waiting around for Adam Hayden to notice me. For the first time since I hit double figures, I'm going to be a real teenager. Wild, fun-loving and ruthless as hell.

Kumara and Lucy have been working on me for what feels like hours, shaping my eyebrows, styling my hair.

Lucy starts to smooth on liquid foundation with a little scrap of sponge. I feel twinges of panic. With each tiny fluttery butterfly stroke she's erasing me, turning me as blank as a Barbie.

Having rubbed out all traces of the old Naomi, Lucy starts to create the new improved version with Added Shimmer; blending here, smudging there. Occasionally, she says crossly, 'Stop frowning,' or hands me a tissue, commanding, 'Blot.'

She steps back and they both inspect me with critical expressions, as if they're deciding how many marks I get out of ten.

'Will I do?' I ask nervously.

Kumara's eyes glint with mischief. 'Can't you tell?'

Suddenly they're jumping up and down, screaming

and hugging me. 'You look *gorgeous*, Naomi! Oh my God, Adam is going to *faint*!'

I stare back at my reflection. All I can see is that I'm different. So different I hardly know myself, which is just as well.

The normal me would never have the courage to wear this clingy little skirt, or kissable vampire make-up.

Lucy dives under her bed and emerges, grinning, with a bottle of cheap cider. 'And now we need a *leetle* tiny something to get us in the mood!'

Carrie-Anne

It was my seventh birthday. I had a cake in the shape of a ballet slipper, covered in soft, pale-pink icing. I was obsessed with dance. I pirouetted and jetted my way through life. I was convinced that my life would end if I didn't go to ballet school. So I nagged my parents day and night to let me go. It wasn't a possibility: Mum had unexpectedly become pregnant with twins. They couldn't afford to send their day-dreaming daughter to private school. I remember that the idea of boarding school became particularly desirable to me when I realized that in four months I'd have two shrivelled red-faced beings, making bad smells and bad noises in the room next to mine.

My party was a mass of excitable girls, rushing around screaming and giggling like fairy-tale fiends. My fingertips were yellow from eating too many cheesy treats. My lips were a carroty colour, dyed by cheap orangeade. I was stupidly expecting my parents to make the big announcement that they'd be sending their beautiful daughter to the Royal Ballet School next term. That some distant aunt had decided to bestow a fortune on the favourite niece she'd heard so much about but never actually met. But all my mother did was clear up the pink paper plates and take down balloons and banners. My father was playing taxi driver, ferrying all my little friends back to their homes. That's when I decided to find the evidence I needed. The proof that my parents had secretly granted me my biggest, brightest wish.

I wasn't allowed into my father's study. The word 'study' was too grand a description for the box room, crammed full of our family junk and papers. But I knew exactly where to look. The important box, the one that had our National Health cards and my parents' exam results in it. I only had to stand on my tiptoes. The box wasn't on the top shelf, hidden safely away from my prying hands.

I pushed the door shut and sat cross-legged on the floor. I emptied the contents onto the carpet, scraps of white and blue paper flying through the air. I began my search through the collection of valuable rubbish. At first it

seemed harmless. A green folder. My father had scrawled '*Birth Certificates*' across the front of it. I sniggered naughtily over the silliness of my parents' middle names. Gloria and Keith. Then I pulled out a certificate and nothing made sense any more. This had to belong to someone else. Someone who shared my birthday. Maybe my father had to look after it, because the police were after this poor girl who wasn't me. Some tragic child named Maya Bird. I rummaged through the folder and found a letter. Reading it made my vision blur. Like an impressionist watercolour, my father's study began to swirl. The letter explained how a baby girl called Maya now belonged to Derek and Karen Harris. Now the baby girl had my name.

I only have vague impressions of what happened after my discovery. Flashes of my mother hiding her face from me as she wept, my father trying to calm her, but for some reason yelling at me. I thought that was strange at the time. That I was being punished, in disgrace, because I'd found out the truth.

Later flashes of my mother holding me so tightly, I can no longer breathe, her jumper leaving an angry red mark on my cheek. *Flash*. She's making my hair wet with her tears. She's begging me to forgive her. Shaking me roughly, trying to make me see that she isn't to blame, that they had meant to tell me when I was older, able to understand. What she didn't see through her tears and grief was that I *did* understand. And it didn't matter. It didn't matter that I wasn't going to ballet school. It didn't matter that my only child status was about to be shattered. It didn't matter that my mother didn't give birth to me. None of it mattered, because I understood that my parents really cared for me. If I could make them this distressed, make them howl like wounded animals, they had to truly love me. And that's all I wanted to know. It seemed so clear and simple back then. I wish I knew when things changed. When I started to doubt my instincts, started to doubt my parents' love.

Naomi

We set off arm in arm, giggling. The cider makes me feel all warm and fuzzy inside.

If anyone was watching we'd just look like three girls going to a party. Like we do this kind of thing all the time.

I turn to Kumara. 'Remember when we used to be the Wonder Girls?'

'God, I'd totally forgotten that!' She hugs me. 'Were we ever that sweet and innocent?'

The Hayden house is in the old part of the town, a large rambling Victorian house with a large rambling garden.

I can feel the beat before we even cross the street. The downstairs windows are open. A babble of voices spills out.

My mouth goes dry. I'm supposed to go in there and flirt and sparkle until sunrise. The thought makes me tired all over. I clutch at Kumara. 'I can't!'

'Naomi, calm down, you're going to have a great time,' she promises.

We go round the back. The kitchen door is open. There are crates of alcohol on the kitchen counter. I dart an involuntary glance at the fridge. No messages. The Haydens must be in a shouting phase.

Lucy removes plastic cups from a stack, fills them sloppily with sparkling wine and hands two to me and Kumara. 'Have fun, girls,' she says in a sexy voice. 'I'm going to find Dan and snog his face off.'

Kumara tows me through the house into a dimly lit room pulsing with music. I get a chaotic impression of moving bodies, some dancing, some lying down, all of them in pairs.

Kumara introduces me to a few of her friends but it's impossible to hear what anyone's saying. After a while she goes off to dance with one of the boys. She turns to smile encouragingly from time to time, but I can tell I'm cramping her style. I wander off, clutching my plastic cup, feeling like a two-year-old who's lost her mum in Woolworths.

I go back and forth between the dancers and the kitchen for what feels like hours, refilling my cup with cheap wine. When I look at my watch, it's barely ten thirty. I remember that I'm meant to be a rebel teen, letting down my hair, so I tentatively join the dancers.

I can dance for hours when I'm by myself, but here it feels as if I'm just pretending.

Finally I can't stand it and go out into the garden.

The minute I hit the fresh air, I feel very strange. Fortunately there's a step. I lower myself carefully, taking slow deep breaths until the garden firms up again.

Actually it's more like a country orchard, with everything running wild and lots of apple trees. The leaves are so pale against the midsummer night that they give off a ghostly moonlight of their own.

I don't see or hear Adam come out. I feel him, as always, through my skin. Now he's here it'll be OK. It will stop being horrible. There'll just be the two of us together.

But he stands there so long without saying anything that I start to sweat. Somehow I've missed a vital cue.

He's expecting me to do or say something but I have no idea what. Eventually he lowers himself beside me, sets a beer bottle down in the grass and lights a cigarette.

It's the first time we've ever been alone together in real life. I'm waiting for him to say something about how he's seen me around. But he just sits there in silence. I steal a sideways look. To my dismay he looks furious. I feel a flash of panic. Adam can't be angry with me yet. He doesn't even know me.

'Are you all right?' I ask anxiously.

He gives a bitter laugh. 'Are you? Is anybody?'

I have no idea what to say next. At last I say desperately, 'Erm, I'm Naomi, by the way.'

'Yeah, Lucy's friend. I know,' he says.

Oh, God, I think, what has she told him?

'You look different.' Adam sounds accusing.

I feel my face burn. 'I put on a little make-up,' I mumble defensively. 'Otherwise I'm the same as usual really.'

'No. You look completely different.' Adam takes a gloomy swig from his bottle, then as an afterthought offers it to me.

'Oh, no, that's OK,' I say hastily. I've become aware of angry voices coming from an upstairs window. Adam glowers with embarrassment. I tell myself it's not me who's making him so angry. It's whatever's happening up there. Without knowing I'm going to, I daringly take the bottle from his hand. 'Perhaps I'll have a sip.'

Inside they're playing a Cyndi Lauper song, 'Time After Time'. The night air smells of honeysuckle. Traffic swooshes past and the moon edges slowly over the apple trees. A skinny little cat is stalking us in the shadows. It seems to want to get close, but at the last minute it always veers away.

Adam sees me looking. 'It's feral,' he says. 'Wild,' he adds, as if I might not know what 'feral' means. 'I put food out sometimes.'

I feel a painful rush of feeling. He's showing me he has a heart. 'I used to have a cat,' I say, barely audibly.

'Used to,' he repeats. 'Did it get run over?'

I shake my head. 'We got rid of him. Mum's boyfriend was allergic.'

'Sounds like an arsehole,' he says.

'He is.'

146

You couldn't call it a conversation. Just halting words with agonizing silences between. But the shy little cat and the moon and the apple trees make it almost romantic; if I could just edit out the vomiting sounds from somewhere near the kitchen door.

Adam's bare arm is so close I can feel warmth rising from his skin. Before tonight, he was just an idea, a dream in my head; now he's real, and I'm not sure I can bear it.

I want to say something deep and insightful, something that shows I understand what he's going through, but everything I say sounds lame.

'Your house is so beautiful,' I get out finally. 'I mean, this garden and everything . . .'

'Yeah, *beautiful*,' he says in a mocking voice. 'A beautiful fucking war zone.'

Maybe he's just been waiting for me to shut up, because suddenly Adam stubs out his cigarette and makes a grab for my shoulder and we're kissing.

I've never kissed a boy before. I suppose I'm expecting something to happen, something that will stop me feeling so gawky and self-conscious, so *separate*.

But if anything it gets worse. Adam's breathing sounds unnaturally loud and wheezy in my ear and there's a smell of cheap wine and cigarettes, and a faintly sour smell which I think might be Adam himself. Also the problem of not knowing how long it's meant to go on. I mean, if I stop now, he might think I don't like him.

I decide to let Adam be the one to stop. At last he does, but I'm not sure if I was doing it right, because he's not even looking at me.

'So do you, er, want to come upstairs?' he says coldly.

The words sounds weird, forced, like he feels he has to say them. He stands up and holds out his hand, still not looking at me.

I don't know why, but it doesn't seem as if I have a choice. I take his hand and we go into the house. –

Someone's dropped a bottle on the kitchen floor. Wine has splattered everywhere and I feel my shoes stick to the kitchen tiles. I check the soles of my shoes for broken glass, and Adam says impatiently, 'Are you coming or what?'

We have to squeeze down the hall past intertwined bodies.

A girl is huddled on the bottom stair, quietly sobbing to herself.

'Sorry,' I mutter, as I squeeze past. The stairs are dark. Without thinking I switch on the light but the bulb pings and goes out.

'Sorry,' I say again and Adam shoots me an incredulous look.

It'll be different inside his room. It'll be like that moment under the apple trees before I messed it up by talking. We'll shut the door and all our awkwardness will be gone. We'll melt together like we do in my daydreams, and the real kissing will start.

I hold his hand and as we climb the stairs in the dark, I see every stair rise and fall in slow motion.

Carrie-Anne

Gemma wants to party harder than she ever has before. Wants to forget about Carl. She wants to get so high she'll be able to touch the stars. Gemma wants to party harder than she ever has before, moving and shaking her body to the delicious beat, pumping her pelvis as though the music is a new and fascinating lover. So we hit the beach and light a beacon to summon the Lord of Misrule. Like worshippers of the black arts, we spin around the fire, entranced by the beat of the dark techno that shakes the sands and turns the tides. I've never taken any drugs before. But Matt has made me feel cold inside and I want to be warm. He says he has some good shit. The little cartoon characters on the tabs make me laugh; the bright and babyish colours make it seem so innocent and I feel stupid chewing the tiny pieces of cardboard. At first I am relieved. Nothing seems to happen. I suppose I had expected instant results. To suddenly see the true face of God, or know the answers to all the big questions. All I get is this slow, fuzzy feeling in my stomach, like a belly full of sherbet. Gradually the fuzziness works its way up my body, twisting in my chest, clawing at the back of my throat and bursting into my head.

Everything, everyone begins to get soft edges; like in a dream I watch my friends shape-shift into different beings, some recognizable, others fantastical. One minute Gem is the Wicked Witch of the West, the next a Monet of dots and colour. The sand begins to pulsate as though it has a heartbeat. When I hold a large pebble to my ear, I can hear it breathing. My heart is speeding. My mouth is dry. I am desperate to keep hold of reality, but the harder I try the further I fall into the trip. My body is full of tingling pins and needles. My hearing has become hollow, as though my brain is searching to hear a sound somewhere beyond the real world, reaching to hear the unspoken secrets of the cosmos. I look over at Gemma. The exhilaration on her face, the excitement, makes me understand she's embraced her Milky Way; she's touched the stars. But no matter how I try to hide from the coldness I feel inside, I can't. If anything it expands. I am desperate to sleep, to wake up and feel

normal again. But when I close my eyes I feel like I am spinning on a roundabout with no control over the disturbing images that fly through my mind. I am falling deeper into the drug and I want out.

When I try to call out to Matt, to anyone, for help, I find I can't speak. In my mind I am positive I am talking rationally, speaking in English. But when I hear the sound coming from my lips I sound like a Teletubby. I desperately want to pee. I manage to crawl to a secluded cove and carefully crouch down, but find I can't urinate. I have to concentrate so hard, but still nothing will happen. My body knows I need to go to the toilet, but my mind won't allow it. In the silence, away from the flames and my friends, I begin to see the sand ripple like an organic being. I see it rise and fall. I am surrounded by sand that is inhaling and exhaling. I run in the wrong direction, away from my friends.

It is not until I am halfway to Penzance that I realize my mistake. The sand has stopped breathing and I feel safe again. I lie down on the damp, gritty sand and look up towards the heavens. It is just before dawn and the clouds have become angels. They drift about the sky; their ragged wings touch the rising sun. I am completely transfixed, and part of me knows

that if I can just focus on this breathtaking celebration of the skies for long enough I'll be OK.

I fall asleep where I lie, and am rudely awoken by two children poking me in the back with their fishing nets. I twist onto my side and pull a silly face that sends them screaming up the beach towards the safety of their parents. I struggle to my feet and feel the back of my head. My hair has become matted with sea-salt and sand. I must look like a mermaid washed up on the beach, finding her land legs for the first time. I hear shouting and turn to see Matt running towards me.

Washing in a bowl of lukewarm water has done nothing to revive me. I'm not going to feel happy until I've spent an hour in a hot power shower.

'Sorry the showers aren't working. Are you feeling better?'

Having Matt so near confuses me. 'I'm fine.'

'Then why did you wander off like that?'

'Why did you shag Gemma?' As soon as I've said it, I want to snatch it back. Pretend I don't know.

Matt sits back on his heels. 'It was nothing.'

'Then why do it?' I pick up my comb and begin to yank

out the tangles. I tug so hard I think my scalp is going to bleed. But the pain distracts me from Matt's guilty expression. Makes me feel like less of a fool for trusting either of my so-called friends. 'I wish you'd both stop calling it nothing. Because it wasn't. It was definitely something. And that something has totally screwed anything we had.'

'Why? It's not like I haven't slept with other girls.'

'I know that. But Gem was— is my best friend. It's like shitting on my doorstep or something. Besides, you knew how I felt about you, otherwise you wouldn't have decided you had to give me that crappy little chat the other night.'

Matt stands up and tries to brush dried mud off his jeans. 'I hate this place. This stuff gets everywhere, even in my teeth.'

'God! You're just like my father. Whenever things get even the slightest bit emotional suddenly the car needs an oil change or the gutters need cleaning—'

Matt cuts me off. 'This isn't up for discussion, Carrie. This isn't your business. Leave it alone. Now I don't know about you but I could do with a massive fry-up. I think I'll head over to the farm and pick myself up some pork.'

That's it. I'm not going to get anything else out of Matt.

Naomi

I walk through the town in my borrowed clothes.

I tell myself, 'That didn't happen.'

When I get home the flat is empty. My mother must be staying over at Maurice's.

I go straight to the bathroom. I empty in the last of Mum's expensive rose bath oil and run both taps until the bath is almost full. The hot water runs out almost immediately, but I don't notice this until I'm actually climbing in, so I climb straight out again, covered in bath foam, my teeth chattering.

Mum has left her fluffy white bathrobe behind the door. I put it on then I crawl into her bed.

I'm not crying, I don't feel much really.

I just keep telling myself, *That didn't happen, it didn't happen, it didn't happen.*

*

I walk around like a sleepwalker for days. Then one morning I wake up to see the sun shining in through my bedroom window and it's like the old Jimmy Cliff song. The rain clouds roll away and I see my life with crystal clarity.

I see that this sleepwalking isn't a new thing. I've been doing it ever since my father moved out. Ever since I was a little girl, desperate for my mother to notice I existed.

One of Lily Macsweeny's sayings pops into my head: *Now is the only time there is.*

I jump out of bed. I'm suddenly galvanized with nervous energy. For the first time ever I've got – not just dreams, but plans. They're so clear I can almost touch them.

In September I'll start A levels. I'll take art and art history and maybe English, then I'll apply for art school somewhere far away from here – Edinburgh or Brighton; some town near the sea where I can breathe.

I'm like a person with a life-threatening illness, who's suddenly terrified of wasting time. I dash down to the library, borrow a pile of books on modern art

156

and shut myself away in my room, reading avidly.

When I return my books to the library a few days later, I take out a set of Italian language tapes. If I take art at A level I'll go to Tuscany with the art class in my first year.

I picture myself walking through the Uffizi Gallery, and later at a street café in Florence, speaking fluent Italian to an attentive waiter. I'm looking slightly mysterious in sunglasses and a little Audrey Hepburn dress, and my life is so full and exciting that if you were to say 'Adam Hayden' to me, I'd have to think twice to place him.

On the way back from the library, I see a card in the window of Café Esmeralda. The café is a new arrival in our town and a definite cut above The Oasis, selling good coffee and genuine French pâtisserie.

I go in and ask the woman inside if she'll give me a job for the summer. She looks me over coolly and says she'll give me a week's trial.

When I come out, I'm thrilled with myself. I run into the first phone box I pass, dial Kumara's number and just say, 'Hi, it's me.'

'Jesus, Nomes!' she screams into the phone. 'Where the hell have you been? After that party you just dropped off the face of the earth!'

'I've been doing some thinking,' I tell her. 'But I'm fine. I'm great!' I tell her about my job and my new boss. 'Marguerite's got to be in her fifties, but she is amazingly stylish, I think it's because she's French.'

Before I hang up, Kumara says, 'Did you hear Lucy split up with Dan?' Afterwards, I realize she didn't mention Adam.

She doesn't know, I think. No one knows.

I don't know what to make of Marguerite. She's so quiet and low-key and she rarely smiles, which makes me feel I must be doing something wrong. At first I am constantly making silly little mistakes. But finally she's satisfied I can meet her exacting standards and we grow more comfortable with each other.

When we're not serving customers, we replenish supplies of salad for the chiller cabinet, whip up egg mayonnaise, or make up lunchtime orders for nearby businesses. And as we work we chat.

Marguerite tells me about her childhood in Paris, her first marriage to a doctor, and about her children, all of whom are grown up and live overseas. I tell her about my childhood travels and how I used to go into Mum's studio just to gaze at her cloud photographs.

'Perhaps you too will be a photographer, Naomi,' she says.

'Oh I'm useless with cameras,' I say. 'All that stuff about f-stops and shutter speeds.'

She gives me one of her shrugs. 'Pouf. These are things any person of intelligence can learn.'

Marguerite's second husband is retired and often drops in around midday to help out with the lunchtime rush. The first time I see them together, I can see immediately that they love each other. They're not being all touchy-feely, just working silently side by side making up baguettes with avocado salad. But when they look at each other, there's this . . . spark. I actually have to look away. I've never seen anything so intimate in my life!

Kumara arrives one afternoon just as we're clearing

up. Marguerite insists that I stop work. She sits us down at a table in the empty café and brings us cappuccinos and two huge slices of *tarte tatin*. Then she turns up the radio. 'So you can talk undisturbed,' she explains in her cool manner.

'God,' sighs Kumara as Marguerite goes back to bagging up the rubbish. 'You have the best job.'

'You should see me with the cappuccino machine,' I boast.

We talk about Kumara's love life, which is not going well, and about her ambition to go to drama school. She's having doubts. 'Do you ever feel like you're this walking teenage cliché, Nomes? I mean, everyone we know has these huge dreams, but what if we all end up staying right here in this town, like our parents?'

'Not me,' I say fiercely. 'I'm leaving first chance I get.'

Her face brightens. 'I nearly forgot – Lucy's having a party tomorrow night. Want to come?'

I shake my head. 'I have to be up early for the breakfast customers.' My tart tastes a bit funny suddenly, almost metallic. I push my plate away.

'You're not on a diet, are you?' Kumara asks.

'I'm just not very hungry.'

'I'll finish it,' she says and greedily helps herself.

Carrie-Anne

'Did Matt manage to catch up with you? He went ballistic when you disappeared last night – we all did.'

Gemma's lying on her back, knees bent, attempting to perform abdominal crunches. We haven't officially made up but both of us are too blasted from the previous night for another round of accusations and home truths. The boxing gloves are off for now.

'God, Gem! How can you do that now? I feel like someone took the top off my skull and inserted a siren. I've never felt so hung over before.'

She scrutinizes my face, then nods. 'You're right, you have the biggest shadows under your eyes. You make a panda look subtle.'

She continues with her vigorous routine. It makes me feel queasy watching her rise up and down, muscles contracting and loosening.

'Did you and Matt get sorted out? Are you guys all cool now about the stupid shag incident?'

I lie down so my head is nestling next to hers. We used to lie like this all the time when we were younger. Picking shapes and faces out of the clouds. Giggling, tickling, being free and happy. But we're not seven years old any more and neither of us is laughing now. I move my body so that there's a distance between us.

'I guess. Not really. There's this big empty space between us.'

'Maybe not for ever though?'

I begin to pick at the dirt embedded under my nails. 'No, it feels permanent. I don't think things will ever be the same. How are things with you and Carl?'

I roll onto my stomach and look over at Gem. Her hair is fine and golden, reminding me of my little Jelly Bean waiting impatiently for me to return.

'It's over, which is shit, but I'll survive.'

'And what about . . . about you know who?'

'Don't worry about that. Matt was just . . . Matt. I really didn't think you'd get that upset.' She sits bolt upright. 'Besides, I always thought you had a little something going

with Carl . . . Come on, you can tell me now he's dumped me.'

When Gemma gets like this it's useless to protest. The more you try to convince her you're not interested, the more excited she gets about the idea that you are. Until in a frenzy she runs off to try and play matchmaker for whichever poor soul she is fixated on.

'Yes, that's it, Gem. I want Carl. Mmmm, I want him so badly!' I'm not ready to share the truth with her. I'm not sure I ever will again.

Gemma turns to face me. Her eyes are full of mischief. 'Really? That's interesting, because—'

I stop her from sharing the little intimacies of her sex life. Sometimes Gemma's sexual adventures completely put me off the idea of ever having a boyfriend. 'Please spare me the details. You're a total slut.'

'And you love me for it. Because it's like that thing, you know? I'm the bad girl, you're the good girl – what is that thing called?'

'You mean I live vicariously through you. You get down and dirty, while I retain my sweetness, my goodness.'

'Yeah, that's the thing. Vicariously, I like that.'

This is one of the stories Gemma has written for us. She is the bad girl whose life is full of sexual intrigue and passion. I am this delicate, refined creature who likes books and homework. In Gem's mind I am like a Barbie doll. I lack the proper equipment.

'Oh, what's happening about your mum? Are you going to meet her?'

Gemma's question brings me down to earth. I'd forgotten my disastrous phone call the previous day. I want to slap myself for being such an idiot. I haven't even checked my phone for messages. I can't put it off. I have to see.

'Hello, Carrie-Anne, it's your dad here. I hope everything's going well in Cornwall. We all miss you here. Your mum wanted me to tell you to make sure you eat some decent food. Um, it's very quiet here without all that loud music you play. I hope you come back soon so I can complain and make you turn it down. Anyway, I'll call again tomorrow. Love you, petal.'

BEEP.

'Hello. Carrie, this is Emma. Mum said I could call and tell you about my ballet lesson. I'm being moved up to the next grade. And I wanted you to know. Mum said it was OK for me to sleep

in your room until you came back. I haven't touched anything, I promise. Oh, and Paddington Bear is very well. Um, I think you should come home now. Mum keeps crying and pretending she's not. And I heard her tell Daddy that she was scared you weren't coming back. Is that true? I love you and—

BEEP.

Hello, Carrie, it's your mum here. Your dad's paid some money into your account . . . just in case.

BEEP.

'Hello, this is a message for Carrie-Anne Harris. I hope I have the right number. I spoke to you yesterday concerning Naomi Bird. I was just calling to let you know she'll be returning sooner than expected. She's in London until tomorrow morning, so she'll be back in Newquay tomorrow evening, if you'd like to call back. Bye.

BEEP.

I didn't think it was really possible for your heart to stop from shock. But mine has. If a surgeon were here, he'd certify me officially dead. I have to deal with the terrifying prospect that tomorrow I could be meeting my biological mother. This life-changing event is about to unfold, and all I can think about is that although I've packed my entire wardrobe, I've completely forgotten clean knickers. If I don't act quickly I'll be forced to meet the woman who formed me and carried me for nine months in her body, wearing dirty underwear.

I spot Carl shaking hands with Jed and patting him on the back in an oddly matey fashion. The little man then shuffles off towards the farmhouse, muttering to the ground on his way. I start a mad sprint over to Carl. 'Help! I need help.' I come to a standstill, puffing hard.

'What's up?'

'I need a ride into town. I totally spaced and forgot to pack any underwear.'

'You want me to take you underwear shopping?' Carl looks horrified.

'You muppet. I just need a lift. And I thought we could get some breakfast.'

Carl looks at his watch. 'Don't you mean lunch? What about the others?'

'Screw 'em. It's been ages since we hung out together.'

Carl scratches the stubble on his chin. 'True – last time

we hit the town together was before Gem and I started going out.'

'So?' I nudge him. 'Can I have that lift?'

'I'm not insured to drive Matt's car.'

'I doubt he is. I doubt it's even his. Come on. You've had your driver's licence for three months and I've never once seen you go anywhere.'

'I don't have any wheels.'

'You do now.' I shake the car keys in his face. 'Don't be a wuss! Like a little criminal activity ever put you off a gag before. Just last night you were popping pills like they were Smarties.'

'They *were* Smarties. I haven't taken drugs for about a month. Need to keep my head clear for the DJing. But as you're practically begging me—'

'I was not begging, you scumbag. Now let's go and buy some pants,' I say, tugging at his sleeve.

Naomi

I am a walking teenage cliché and I don't even know it.

I utterly fail to put two and two together. I tell myself I must just be getting super-sensitive for some reason. These days, just the smell of potatoes boiling in a pan fills me with actual physical disgust. Yet I have an intense craving for watercress, which I normally hate.

I'm not just super-sensitive to food. One day a Cyndi Lauper song comes on the radio in the café and my ears start buzzing and I almost black out.

One night I go back to Kumara's house after work. Kumara's cooking me supper. I'm finally going to see her heart-throb Judd Nelson in *The Breakfast Club*.

It's the first time I've been to the Macsweenys' since Mum and Lily broke friends. When I walk through their front door, a wave of violent homesickness washes over me. The house is so familiar, I feel as if I've stepped back

169

in time. I half expect to see three little girls in swirly capes and bullet-deflecting cuffs.

Kumara proudly shows me Lily's study area on the upstairs landing, with its desk and anglepoise lamp and shelves filled with law books and box files. But I know that the new lawyer Lily is basically the same person because she has a quote from an ancient Persian poet pinned up on her notice board.

Kumara makes chicken salad, but I'm feeling so mixed up inside, I hardly eat anything. The whole time we're watching the movie, I'm getting more and more upset. At the end, when Molly Ringwald, the school princess, gives her earring to good-looking but dangerous Judd Nelson, I burst into tears.

'Nomes, what is it?' says Kumara in alarm. 'What's wrong?' She rushes off, coming back with yards of toilet roll, and I mop myself up.

'Sorry,' I gasp. 'Don't know what came over me.'

My friend puts her arm around me. 'Did something happen with Adam? I've noticed you never talk about him now.'

I shake my head. 'I was crying at the film, that's all.'

Kumara is baffled. 'But it's got such a feel-good ending!'

I try to laugh. 'Oh, just ignore me! I'm always like this before my period. One time I cried over a Marathon advert.'

The Breakfast Club is Kumara's favourite film so I can't tell her how miserable I felt, seeing those American teenagers sitting around exposing their secret wounds to each other. I can't tell her that it's only in films that talking makes things better. In real life it just makes them much much worse.

My body has suddenly developed a bewildering life of its own. Overnight, my breasts inflate into miniature torpedoes. The lightest pressure from clothes makes them sting and burn. When I tie on my apron at work I catch myself wincing with pain.

I used to love my job, but now I have to drag myself through the working day, desperately trying not to inhale the smell of hard-boiled eggs and tuna.

I'm tired all the time. When I'm not tired, I'm queasy, and when I'm not queasy, I'm famished. This is not normal hunger. It's like I'll actually die if I don't eat. This ferocious need for food can strike at any time, even when I'm asleep.

One night I wake and immediately I'm mentally scanning the contents of our fridge. I remember that Marguerite sent me home with a carton of home-made pea soup. Instantly I'm a girl possessed. I have to have that soup *now*.

I creep into the kitchen in my pyjamas, take the soup out of the fridge, stealthily pour it into a saucepan and turn on the gas ring. While my soup is heating, I make toast and butter the slices thickly. My stomach growls. My mouth waters unbearably. I've just taken a big fabulously satisfying bite of toast when the light snaps on in the hall. I freeze with my mouth full.

My mother comes in, doing up her dressing gown. 'It's three a.m.,' she says. 'What the hell are you doing in here?'

'I didn't mean to wake you. I couldn't sleep and I thought I'd make a snack.'

She folds her arms. 'A hot drink and a biscuit is one thing, but eating pea soup in the middle of the night, that's bizarre behaviour, Naomi!'

'It isn't bizarre at all. I was just really hungry.'

I see her expression change. 'Jesus, when did you last have a period?'

'Mum, calm down, I wanted some soup, that's all. It doesn't mean I'm pregnant. Remember that time you got up and made lemon meringue pie in the middle of the night?'

She's talking over me. 'Stand up! Stand up and let me look at you!' she barks.

'God, does everything have to be this big drama?' I say. 'Can't you just leave me alone?' I try to go on eating, but my hand starts to shake and I'm spilling soup everywhere.

Mum's voice is like a whip. 'Just stand up, Naomi, please, so I can have a proper look at you.'

The kitchen is suddenly churning with violent emotions. I'm terrified. My mother is about to unleash some terrible genie from its bottle and we'll never be able to get it back inside.

I stand up and she looks me over from head to toe. We both stare at the washed-out T-shirt fabric stretched across my scary torpedo breasts. All those years when I longed for my mother to see me, to really see me. Now it's happening and I feel like livestock.

Mum sits down and puts her head in her hands. 'Christ,' she says. 'Jesus Christ, you stupid little cow, how could you do this to me?'

Carrie-Anne

'You twat! You shagged her while she was still with me.'

Matt's nose is gushing with blood. I wish I'd kept my mouth shut. All I wanted was to have someone understand my pain.

'Er . . . hello! You never owned me.'

'Shut up, Gem. I knew you were sleeping around behind my back, but you could at least have had a little bit of respect for me and done it further from home.'

'That's exactly what *I* said.' I can't stop myself joining in and immediately wish I hadn't – Matt's expression makes me want to crumple up like burning plastic and melt into the ground.

'Thanks for opening your fat mouth, Carrie.' Gem is trying not to cry in front of Carl. One of her many cardinal rules concerning the opposite sex is that you never cry when they can see you, unless it is for effect.

'I didn't know it was a secret.'

Gem just shakes her head in disgust. 'This is exactly what I was talking about the other night. Always having to be the centre of attention. Don't pretend you didn't know what would happen.'

Guilt hits me like a wave of nausea. I had wanted this. Gem is right.

'I wasn't thinking.'

'That's obvious.'

'Don't make this about Carrie, Gem. She wasn't the one fucking Matt behind my back.'

'It was *once*! And we were practically over.'

Carl turns to Matt. 'Sorry about that, mate. But I had to do it. We'd better go and get that claret off your face.'

'No problem. I'd have done the same myself.'

'Oh, right, so you forgive him.' Gem is losing her battle with her tears.

'He's my mate. You were only my girlfriend. And now you're not that, you're . . . nothing.'

'But what about us?' Gem is openly sobbing. 'What about this?'

'What are you talking about?'

'The four of us.' She blows her nose hard. 'For a year it's always been you, me, Matt and Carrie-Anne.'

None of us can look at Gem. We can't even look at each other. We walk off in separate directions, to separate spaces, towards separate lives.

It is three o'clock in the morning. Earlier this evening I had Carl rushing around as if I was a gunshot victim in an episode of *ER*. My insides blown wide open, so the doctors and nurses can fall in and out of love over my dying body. He too has suffered from Gem's betrayal, but I am the one uncontrollably sobbing my heart out. Gem has joined us briefly, but it is mainly for Carl's benefit. Gemma suffers from Emotional Deficit Disorder. She can only handle someone's pain and uncertainty for so long. It is three o'clock in the morning and my bottom has gone numb from sitting on cold, unyielding ground. It is three o'clock in the morning – how can I sleep when I have such momentous decisions to make? My mind is like the calm before the storm. I feel uncharacteristically rational. It is the same old pattern with me. Whenever I get close to something I've longed for, when I know it is just round the

corner waiting for me to claim it, I freak out and run in the opposite direction. It's scary to think we might actually get what we wish for. It's so much easier imagining it, playing out scenes in your head. In your mind you always have the power to hit REWIND and start over again.

It is three o'clock in the morning and perhaps it isn't rationality I am experiencing. Perhaps it is denial. If I stay level headed, if I remember to keep breathing, I'll fool my body and mind into thinking this is all a daydream. Denial is essential to my adolescent nature. I know I'm not ready, prepared enough to meet my biological mother. It is like a test I haven't revised for; I haven't even seen the syllabus. Deep down I recognize the shame I've been trying to conceal. What if my mother doesn't like me? It is three o'clock in the morning and I've been what-iffing since midnight. The bossy voice inside that tells me I'm no good has surfaced. Telling me I'm one of life's losers. That I'm not special after all, I am just like everyone else, regular. The voice that tells me the reason my mother gave me up for adoption, the reason why my family and friends find it so hard to love me, is that they see my true face. The face

I try to avoid when I look in the mirror. The face that betrays who and what I really am. Judgemental, vicious and selfish.

Naomi

The doctor sits back, looking tired. 'I'm assuming this wasn't planned,' she says wearily.

I shake my head – no.

She sighs. 'Luckily it's not the end of the world at this stage. You're eight weeks pregnant at most so it's a relatively simple—'

I interrupt. 'Don't tell me to have an abortion, because I'm not going to.'

She takes a breath. 'Is your objection on religious grounds?'

'I don't know about religion. I just can't . . . kill my baby.'

'You do know, Naomi, that it's not a real baby yet, just a cluster of cells.'

'It's the size of a bean,' I blurt out.

'Sorry?'

'I looked it up in the library. I'm eight weeks pregnant. My baby is the size of a bean and it's starting to grow fingers. It's not some anonymous blob of jelly.'

'Naomi, in an ideal world, no one in their right mind would have an abortion. But it's not an ideal world and you're only fifteen. Do you honestly want your entire future to be derailed by one little mistake?'

'She's not a mistake, she's a miracle.' My voice shakes and I notice with surprise that my baby has mysteriously become *she*, not *it*.

Her expression is suddenly concerned. 'You're actually planning to keep this baby? Naomi, have you any idea what you'd be taking on?'

'Schoolgirls have babies all the time,' I say.

She takes off her glasses and sighs. 'They certainly do, my dear. And they drop out of school and get dead-end jobs and a lot of them end up coming to me for tranquillizers.'

'Do they start using heroin too and forget how to read?'

I'm making it difficult for her to like me. She takes a breath. 'I'm just saying it will be terribly hard. You're

181

still at school. Have you thought how you'll manage?'

'Mum's really happy to help. She works at home. She's an artist, so her time is pretty flexible.'

I'm stunned with gratitude at Mum's turn-around. She would have come to see the doctor with me, but I wanted to go by myself.

The doctor shuffles my notes and puts them back in the folder. Her way of showing she's giving up on me. 'And this is really what you want?'

'Yes,' I say. 'It's what I want.'

I get up to leave. I'm trembling.

'How'd it go?' my mother asks when I get back. 'Did the old battle-axe give you a hard time?'

I shrug. 'Not really. Hey, you're looking at baby patterns!' I feel a rush of happiness. It was natural that Mum should be shocked at first. But it seems as if she's genuinely warming to the idea of being a granny.

She pats the sofa cushion. 'Come and look at this little jacket – isn't it gorgeous?'

I sit down beside her but I don't look at the pattern. I lean my head against my mother's shoulder. Tears of relief seep out from under my eyelids. 'You're really not angry any more?' I whisper.

'No, sweetie, we are going to be there for you, I promise.'

It's so wonderful to feel safe again that I instantly edit out that puzzling 'we'.

Mum's voice is dreamy, almost singsong. 'I was so young when I had you, darling. Too young to see what a precious opportunity I'd been given. In a way this is like a second chance.'

I try to smile but something feels slightly off.

'I'm only in my thirties. Theoretically I could still have a baby of my own.' Mum laughs. 'Maurice says people will naturally assume it's ours.'

I'm off the sofa in a flash. 'You told Maurice!'

'Of course, sweetie. You can't expect me to keep secrets from the man I love!'

I can hardly get the words out. 'But – but it's got nothing to do with him.'

'It has everything to do with him. Be realistic, Naomi. It's not every man that would take on another man's teenage daughter, let alone a girl with an illegitimate baby.'

There's a buzzing in my ears, like the time Cindy Lauper came on the radio. I'm scared I'm really going to faint but my mother doesn't notice.

'I was incredibly creative when I was expecting you,' she's saying. 'I don't think I've ever taken such good photographs before or since.' She smiles at me but it's not me she's seeing at all. She's imagining her future with Maurice and a beautiful little baby. I've already been airbrushed out of the picture. 'Yes,' she murmurs to herself. 'This is a new start for me, Naomi, a completely new start.'

I wait, barely keeping myself together, until my mother leaves to spend the night at Maurice's. Then I call a taxi and throw things frantically into a bag.

I pay the driver and walk up the garden path to the front door and ring the bell. It's a warm summer evening and the windows are open. I can hear music coming from inside.

This is my last chance. Suppose she sends me away?

Lily comes to the door. Her curly hair has acquired a broad grey streak, and she has reading glasses perched on the end of her nose. She whips the glasses off and I see the marks they've left behind.

'I'm sorry,' I whisper. 'I didn't have anywhere to—'

Lily takes in my tear-stained face and my suitcase and just holds out her arms.

Carrie-Anne

'Why can't you tell me?' I am still wiping sleep out of my eyes as we head down into Newquay. Seven in the morning, the bass booming out loud. I imagine us leaving a cracked road in the wake of our speakers.

'Come on, what's the big secret? What's so important you had to snatch me away from my precious beauty sleep?'

Carl snorts. 'I think you can sacrifice a little of that beauty sleep now and again, gorgeous. Besides, I doubt very much you were actually catching any Zs. How could you, with all this stuff happening today? I know you.'

'Yes, that's great, Carl. But you haven't answered my question.'

'And I don't intend to until we get there.'

Carl is a tease when it comes to secrets. He can hold out for months, managing not to divulge the merest hint of a clue. I have to sit brooding over my unfulfilled curiosity all

the way into town. We finally come to a standstill in a car park.

'Come on, Carl, what are we doing here?'

He stretches his arm out around the back of my seat, his hand brushing my shoulder, sending tingly sensations into my stomach.

'I thought we'd do some sightseeing. Check out the area.'

'Sightseeing? What about the others?'

'They're being idiots. Anyway it's been pure time since I've treated you to ice cream.'

I adjust myself in the seat until I'm facing him. 'Strawberry ice cream?'

'Anything you desire, my lady,' he says.

'Mmm. Can I get a flake too?'

He furrows his brow. 'Well, that may cost you.'

Playing along, I purse my lips and cross my arms. 'OK, how much?'

'Well, a whole chocolate flake ain't cheap. I'd say . . . three smiles and one chuckle – maybe two.'

'Two chuckles! You drive a hard bargain.'

He opens the car door. 'Come on, let's go and explore.'

It is like being a child again. I feel liberated from all the

anxieties and confusions that have been plaguing me. The tacky gift shops selling sticks of rock and fishing nets are once again like treasure troves to us. We buy a fluorescent green bucket-and-spade set and build a city of sand on the beach. Sitting back on our heels we survey our handiwork.

'I haven't built a sandcastle for years. Dad and I always used to make these amazing constructions with moats leading down to the sea. Those were good times.' I look over at Carl. 'Thanks for this.'

'Not a problem. What next? Fish and chips?'

I fall back on the sand, moaning. 'No more food! The ice cream and doughnuts are still working their way through my gut. Besides, it's way too early for lunch.'

'But it's not too early for a pint.'

'It's never too early for you.'

'Fancy finding a pub and having a few drinks then?'

I sit up. 'I have a better idea.'

'Better than sipping cold beer with the baking sun on your back?'

'Come on,' I say, stretching out my hand. 'Let's go.'

I don't know where the idea sprang from. It just seems right.

* * *

'Is this it, Carrie? Check the address again.'

I look down at the piece of paper I am holding in my sweaty hands. 'It's number twelve. Park here, then we can get a better view.'

Carl pulls over and switches off the engine. 'Looks a bit run down – kind of reminds me of my house.'

I like the look of Naomi's house; it almost seems familiar. 'Maybe a bit more bohemian than the Legoland I live in, but I think it has character.'

'Is that a CND sticker in the window?'

I peer out through the windscreen. 'Looks like it. Shit, do you think she's some hippy-dippy space cadet?'

'Probably – would explain where you got it from.'

I lean back in my seat. I can't believe I am really parked on the street where my biological mum lives. She's walked on these pavements. She really exists here.

'What do you think she looks like? Think she looks like you?'

'I don't know. They didn't give me a photo of her, just a vague description. I have to remind myself she's not sixteen any more. She's a grown-up.'

'Like your mum.'

'Nothing like Mum. *She'd* never tolerate the peeling paint on the front door. And she'd have a coronary if our windows ever got that dirty. No, nothing like Karen Harris; probably more like your mother.'

'God, don't wish that on anyone.' Carl lights a cigarette. 'She's never there. Even when she is, she isn't. Her brain's rotted – too much drugs and booze.'

I glance over at Carl. 'For real? I never know when you're telling the truth.'

'I'm serious. It's like having a conversation with a corpse. Sometimes I think she doesn't remember who I am. She looks at me and I see the puzzlement in her eyes, like "Who the hell are you?" That's one of the reasons I'm moving down here – can't handle it any more.' He stubs his cigarette out in the ashtray and lights another. 'But hey, that's life.'

'Can I have one of those?'

'You don't smoke.'

'I know, but maybe I should. I'm really stressed out.'

'I wouldn't advise taking up this particular habit. I think you look like her.'

'What?'

'I reckon you take after your mum.'

'I guess we'll soon see.'

I watch Carl blow smoke rings into the air.

'Why do you think Matt . . . you know?'

'I don't know. To be honest he's been acting like an arse lately.'

'But it feels like it's aimed at me. He knew how much this whole thing with Gem would hurt me.'

Carl brushes some cigarette ash off his jeans. 'It's not just you; he's being strange with us all. I know he was getting weirded out about you wanting more from him.'

I can feel my face turning red with humiliation. I wish I could dissolve into nothing like an aspirin hitting water. 'We did talk about something like that. But he got the whole thing wrong, I was never interested in him like that.' I can feel Carl staring at me, but I can't meet his eyes. I can only imagine what Matt has said. I don't want to hear how he talked to Carl about my clumsy attempts at seduction, the 'Yuck – how repulsive, the idea of shagging Carrie-Anne.'

'Don't worry – he didn't say anything bad about you. And if it makes you feel any better, I told him he was crazy not to want you.'

'You did!' I practically get whiplash turning to look at him. 'You said that?'

'Yeah, I did. Matt has crap taste in women.'

'Thank you. It was sweet of you to defend my . . . my cuteness.'

'Any time. You ready to go?'

'Yeah, it's not like Naomi's suddenly going to appear right now.'

'OK, I have one secret stop to make before we head back to the campsite.'

I unfasten my seat belt. 'Just give me a minute, there's one thing I want to do.'

I get out and walk towards the house. I want to touch something that I know Naomi has touched. I walk softly up the garden path, picking my way carefully over the tufts of grass and dandelions sprouting in the gravel. I walk up to the front door. I am afraid to breathe or even blink. My hand shaking, I reach out and touch the doorknob.

Carl parks outside a huge Georgian-style building. 'Well? What do you think?' he says, yanking the hand brake on.

'It's a house. What about it?'

Carl takes a set of keys out of his pocket. 'Want to come and see?'

The lobby is full of old flyers, phone directories and peeling paint.

'What can I say, Carl? It's . . . it's very you.'

'No, Carrie-Anne, this is shit. Wait till we get upstairs.'

He runs up the staircase, and I obediently follow. He stops in front of a blue door. The recurring theme for the area is clearly peeling paint. I can see the orange beneath the cobalt peeping through. Carl unlocks the door and we enter the most magnificent room. The ceiling is so high, Michelangelo's fingers would have itched to paint it like the heavens.

'This is what I wanted you to see. Welcome to my new home.'

'You're moving here? How can you afford this? It's huge.' I'm beginning to shake.

'This room is the only room, besides a kitchen that makes a cardboard box look big, and a shared bathroom that's even smaller. But I'm not complaining, it's just the start. It's all thanks to my new best friend Jed.'

'Ah, the vertically challenged campsite manager. Should have known you were up to something.'

'Yeah, well, Jed's uncle owns this building so I'm getting a reduced rate for the first six months.'

'You lucky bastard! So when do you move in?'

'Now, if I like. And the really cool thing is that when you come and visit your mum, you can hang here.'

I thought Matt was the only one who could make my bellybutton tingle. I feel confused. I have to get out of the flat before I start to compromise my sparkly, spanking clean reputation.

'Well, we should head back to the others.'

'Yeah, you're right. What say we all come back here post mother meeting and do a little partying?'

'Sounds good to me.'

Naomi

I'm just staying with them until the baby's born – that's what we're telling everyone.

Lily spends hours on the phone talking to officials, and a social worker comes to see me. Eventually it's arranged that I can transfer to Ruby and Kumara's school to do my A levels.

'Everyone at our school is going to adore you,' says Ruby.

I laugh disbelievingly. 'Even when I'm hugely pregnant?'

She gives me a wicked grin. 'Absolutely. You'll have novelty value.'

Kumara has her head in the wardrobe, as she makes space for my things. 'And if some moron tries to give you a hard time, just shout and me and Lucy will sort them out for you,' she calls.

'They'll just be jealous because you've made love and they didn't,' says Ruby fiercely.

She's only fourteen so I don't say that I haven't yet made love with anyone. What I did was have inept sex which, as Marguerite cheerfully remarked, any fool can do.

Ruby sits beside me on the bed. 'May I?' she says.

'Sure, go ahead.'

She puts her hand reverently on my stomach.

'I won't feel movements for another couple of months, the midwife says,' I tell her.

Like Kumara, Ruby now wears black twenty-four hours a day. With her green eyes and her mother's luminous skin, she looks like an apprentice witch as she traces the swelling curve of my belly with an awed expression. She looks up and her eyes are shining. 'Do you think she can hear us talking?'

Ruby thinks you're a girl too.

'Maybe,' I say.

Ruby jumps up and starts searching eagerly through Kumara's tapes. 'We should play her The Cult every day so she'll grow up really cool.'

Lily comes in with some clean towels. 'Really deaf more like,' she says.

Kumara emerges from the wardrobe and squashes up beside me and Ruby. They both put their arms around me. 'Welcome home, Nomes,' Kumara says. 'We've missed you.'

'You're going to be a brilliant mother,' says Ruby. 'We'll all help you bring her up, won't we, Mum?'

Lily's on her way out of the room, but she stops and says, 'We'll support Naomi to do whatever she decides.'

'That's what I said, birdbrain,' says Ruby cheerfully. 'Honestly, Mum, you talk just like a social worker sometimes.'

A month later, I'm coming out of the doctor's when I hear someone call my name.

I turn to see a tired-looking girl with an expensive baby buggy smiling expectantly.

At last it clicks. 'God, Verity Meadows! What are you doing here?'

She looks shy. 'I had to take Leo for his jabs. He was so good, just gave the tiniest little whimper. Now he's crashed out.' She smiles down at the sleeping baby.

I'm not sure I've understood properly. 'Leo isn't your—?'

'Yes,' she says, 'he's my little boy.'

To my eyes he looks more like a tiny shrivelled old man than a baby, but I say dutifully, 'He's gorgeous.'

'He was a bit of a surprise,' she admits. 'But like my dad says, now Leo's here, we have to make the best of it. I've been so lucky. Mum and Dad found me this little flat, so I'm completely independent.'

'What about your boyfriend?'

She shakes her head. 'It's just me and Leo now.'

'So, erm, how old is your little boy?' I ask.

'Three months,' she says. 'He's just started on proper solids.'

I take a breath and blurt out, 'I'm pregnant too.'

Verity's face changes. 'You're not.'

'I just had my first antenatal appointment. I heard her heartbeat. It sounds so fast, like a herd of galloping horses!'

Her eyes light up. 'But this is so great! We can do baby stuff together and everything.'

'Yes, definitely,' I say.

Verity only lives round the corner so I go back with her to admire her flat. First we stop off at the corner shop and Verity buys exactly two jars of baby food. 'One for Leo's dinner and one for his pudding,' she explains.

Verity lives over a Chinese takeaway. I help her up the flight of stairs with the buggy and she lets us into what she says is a studio flat, but it's really just a bedsitter.

A rear window looks out onto some kind of air vent belonging to the takeaway. The huge silver pipe blocks out almost all the light.

'I'll leave him in his buggy or he'll wake up and want his dinner,' Verity says. 'This way we'll get a few minutes to talk.' She bustles around the kitchen end of her tiny flat, making coffee.

I perch on the sofa. It occurs to me that I don't really know her that well. The last time we had a conversation we both wore white ankle socks.

'Sorry it's a mess,' she calls. 'I meant to vacuum before I went out.'

I look around the spotless room. The carpet and furniture are so pristine they seem totally unused. 'I was just wondering how you keep everything so tidy,' I say.

If I didn't know better, I'd think no one actually lived here. I stealthily inspect the gleaming shelves, hoping to catch a glimpse of a book or a music tape, anything to indicate that Verity still has a life, but there's just a TV, a video and a basket of baby toys.

She comes over with our mugs and a plate of biscuits on a tray. 'You're my first proper visitor actually. So what do you think of my place?' she asks brightly. 'Lovely, isn't it?'

'Yeah, you're so lucky,' I say.

'Mum and Dad wanted me to be independent, but we see them loads. We go over every Sunday to have our dinner. They've kept my old room for me, so we can even stay the night if I like.'

'Do you still have stars on the ceiling?' I ask impulsively.

She gives me a strange look. 'Naomi, that was years ago. We were little girls then.'

Leo starts to grizzle and Verity jumps up. 'Excuse me.'

She opens a jar of baby food, and sets it in a pan of water on the hob. While it's warming up, she unstraps

200

Leo and walks up and down with him, trying to stop him crying.

'Whatever do you do all day?' The question bursts out before I can stop it

Verity looks offended. 'Look after Leo, of course.' She has to raise her voice over his yells. 'Babies are a fulltime job. I give him his bottle five or six times a day, change him, bath him, get up for him in the night. I have to wash his clothes, obviously. And when he's sleeping, I try to keep our home nice.' She laughs. 'I don't know if you remember, but my mum has really high standards. I'd never hear the end of it if I let things slip.'

I try to laugh. 'I suppose.'

Verity sets Leo in his Mothercare baby chair, ties a clean bib around his neck and starts spooning orange gloop into his mouth.

I feel Verity's shiny little flat closing in around me. I go to look out at the air vent. 'So, do you manage to get out much?' I ask casually.

'Oh, yes, I go out every day. We go for lovely long walks together, don't we, Leo?'

I swallow. 'I meant in the evenings – you know, to have

fun with friends.'

The view is really depressing me so I go back to the sofa.

'To be honest I've sort of lost touch with people from school. But if I want company I can always phone Mum or put the TV on, and I've got Leo of course. We have lovely times, don't we?' she asks him in her new bright voice as she scrapes carrot purée off his chin.

I know I should let it go but I can't. 'It must get lonely. I mean, he's a gorgeous little boy, Verity, but don't you ever feel just a bit, you know, *trapped*?'

Verity stares out at some invisible country on the other side of the air vent and her expression is so bleak I feel my heart turn over.

'Leo didn't ask to be born, Naomi,' she says quietly. 'He's just an innocent little baby. I'm all he's got.'

When I get back to Lily's house, everyone else is out.

I lie on my bed and shut my eyes. I can feel the new fluttery sensation behind my ribs which means you're awake in there, and I think of art school and Italy and all the other places I haven't seen.

Lately, whether I'm standing, sitting or lying down, my hands gravitate to you, as if you're magnetic. But this time I lift up my top and stroke my belly, and I picture you kicking and turning inside me like a tiny astronaut and I start to cry.

I'm crying because you're a miracle and not a mistake, and you deserve a real family, not a scared girl heating up baby food in a bedsit with just a TV for company. I'm crying because I'm only sixteen and I haven't lived yet and I still want the moon and the stars and I'm just not ready, I'm not ready, I'm not ready . . .

Carrie-Anne

'Where did you guys get to?'

'Nowhere, nothing, why?'

It's one o'clock in the afternoon, but Gemma has more glitter and glitz on her than a Soho drag queen.

'What's the occasion?' I decide to make-believe that Gem and I are still friends for ever. Maybe if I pretend hard enough we will be.

'Didn't you hear? There's this Radio One party on the beach. And I also want Carl to see what he's missing out on. There are going to be some serious hotties there and my pulling power is peaking.'

'That was a quick recovery.'

'I'm only sixteen, Carrie. It's not like Carl and I were a step away from marriage. I'm young, fun and hopefully soon will be full of rum.' Gem starts to brush her hair. 'I just know I'm going to get spotted today. My stars in

Elle were really good for this month.'

Gemma's convinced she's only a skip and a hop away from supermodel stardom. She spends her weekends strutting around the streets and clubs of our town, waiting for that moment when her real life, existing only on the pages of a glossy magazine, will start.

'Well, you look good enough to eat. So if there are any talent spotters around, I'm sure you'll get picked.'

I'm not lying for once. Gemma has superstar written all over her. She just needs a camera to flash and she's all pearly whites and bouncy blonde hair.

'I hope you're right, Carrie. I need this to happen soon. School finishes in a few months. If I don't have something lined up my mum's going to be marching me down to Dad's office. I'm not like you. I don't have a brain. I just have a bod. God, something has to rescue me from this nightmare life.'

It would never occur to Gemma that maybe she can do it on her own. She is always waiting for someone else to shoot in and make it all better.

'So how long until *the meeting*?'

'Who knows? I guess I may not hear anything until, like, seven or eight. Maybe not till tomorrow.'

'Bummer. Are you going to join us for the gig later?'

'Don't see why not. I have my mobile charged up and switched on. I don't want to sit here all day, while you guys are out having fun.'

'Cool. But you're going to have to change if you want to stand within a mile radius of me. I mean, hello! *Old School* is so last season! I'm into *Hollywood Chic* now.'

A party on the beach is just the distraction I need. My sudden excitement at all things Carl-orientated almost makes me forget that my life is probably going to end in a few hours.

Watching Gem working her stuff on the male members of the crowd is more entertaining than the DJ's high-pitched squealing on the stage. Gem doesn't believe in mystery or playing hard to get, or even slightly difficult to get. She sticks out her padded bosom and wriggles her peachy bottom until perspiration appears on her forehead. She is trying so hard it makes me wince.

'I don't get it, Carrie-Anne. What's wrong with these guys? Do you think we've accidentally stumbled on a Gay Pride rally? Am I not, like, totally scintillating?'

'You look so hot. There are plenty of guys here who are just drooling over you.'

'Well I don't want just any guy.'

She disappears into the crowd. I've only been here ten minutes and I'm already beginning to wish I wasn't. Everyone is having such a good time; their happy faces seem deliberately aimed at me: '*Look at me, Carrie-Anne, I know how to enjoy myself. I know how to be a proper teenager. Why don't you?*' Even Carl is lost in the sea of blissful bodies. I am surrounded by thousands of people and I've never felt so lonely. It's only three o'clock. I'm not sure I can survive the next few hours without bursting from emotional overload. I still have time to make a Houdini-type exit. My birth mother will be none the wiser and I can keep the fiction that surrounds her alive in my mind. In fact I'm beginning to debate whether I have anything to gain from meeting her except for years of therapy. I'm so desperate to back down, to be told that I am allowed to return to my rambling old house, that I do what all respectable ETs do: I move away from the crowd and phone home.

'Hello, this is the Harris residence, how may I help you?'

It's my mum.

'Hi, it's me.'

There's a silence and I check my phone to make sure I'm still connected. 'Hello?'

'Yes, I can hear you. I'm here. Well?'

'Well what?' We've both slipped effortlessly into defence mode.

'Have you seen *her* yet?'

'No.' I don't know what to say next. How to let her know she's won.

'When?'

'Not sure. Mum, I think you're right.'

'About what?'

'About *this*. Being here.' I don't mean to sound so aggressive. I don't want this conversation to end like all the others: doors slammed, phones flung across the room. 'I'm sorry. I didn't mean to sound so harsh. I'm not angry. I don't remember why I'm here.'

'Why are you asking me?' I can't detect what my mother is feeling or thinking. Her voice is unusually neutral, toneless.

'I'd better go. The others will be wondering where I got to.'

'OK, Carrie.'

I feel the familiar ache of desperation. Have I lost yet another mother? What can I say that will make it all right again? Suddenly it all becomes very simple. I've been struggling for so long to find a way to say sorry, to find a way back into my mother's arms. Finally I know what words to say.

'I love you, Mum. You know that, right?'

I hear her catch a breath on the other end of the phone. I try to picture her face; remember the effect those words used to have.

'I know you do. I love you too. You're my heart. Sometimes I don't like the way you behave, but it doesn't mean I don't care. Perhaps if we said it more often, we'd—'

'For sure, Mum. But I'm still me and you'll always be you.'

'I wouldn't expect anything less, sweetheart. Believe it or not, I was worse at your age.'

'Really?!' I'm stunned that my mum's selective memory has allowed her to recall a time when she wasn't so perfect and conforming.

'Don't sound so surprised, I was known as a bit of a "wild child" in the neighbourhood.'

I laugh, trying to picture my mother as rebellious and free spirited.

'But that's not a story for now,' she says briskly.

'Mum, if I chicken out of this, would that be OK?'

'Of course! There's always tomorrow, or next month, or next year. She . . . Naomi may have given you life, but your spirit is all your own, Carrie – that's unshakeable.'

I am back in her embrace and it feels warm and safe.

'Anyway, Carrie, your dad and I will no doubt be footing this enormous mobile bill next month, so I'd better go. Are you all right now?'

'Yep! For a while anyway. Love to everyone there.'

'OK, love, see you in a few days.'

Have Mum and I just had a conversation without accusations and hurt? Maybe I have grown up. Maybe we both have.

I hear the click of a cigarette lighter behind me, followed by the satisfied sigh of Matt.

'You missed The Dubaholics. Who were you on the phone to?'

'Shit! I didn't even know they were on the line-up.'

'I tried to find you, but you'd done one of your vanishing acts. Who were you on the phone to?' he persists.

'My mum.'

'Which one?'

'I only have one.'

Matt raises an eyebrow. 'Is this good news or bad?'

'It's a ceasefire – for now, anyway.'

'A ceasefire . . . that's good to hear. You used to be close. And no offence, but all that stamping around in a rage was getting boring. You're too old for tantrums, it's just not sexy.'

I dive on him like a kid, tackling him to the ground.

'Who's your daddy?' I cackle. Matt is mad ticklish and I am taking full advantage. 'Come on, who's your daddy?'

'You are! Stop before I piss myself.'

I roll off, flushed and forgiving. If Mum can let my appalling bouts of misbehaviour go, so can I for Matt.

'Mates?' he asks, extending his hand.

'Yeah, mates.' I grasp his hand and shake it hard.

'As we're all matey again, are you going to tell me what's going on between you and Carl?'

I scramble to my feet and smooth down my unruly hair. 'Don't push it. I haven't completely forgiven you yet.'

'Oh come on, don't leave me hanging.'

'No. It's none of your business.' I place my hands on my hips with as much attitude as I can muster. 'Let's just say it's a work in progress.'

'Well, whatever is or isn't going on, I hope it works out for you. Still waiting for your bio— for Naomi to call?'

'Yep. Not sure she'll even bother to.'

'She'll call. And when she does we'll go together, if you want. You're not alone. Now I'm heading back to the beach because this is all getting too pink and girly for me. I'm not good with all these feelings and shit.'

'We're like those kids in that film.'

'What kids in what film?'

'You know. The one where they're all on Saturday detention?'

'Right. The one with that girl with the really big teeth. *The Breakfast Club*!'

'That's the one.'

'I hope not. Bunch of whingy big crybabies, sitting around complaining about being too pretty, too rich, too popular. I hated that film.'

'Oh please, you cried just as much as me when Molly Ringwald gave Judd Nelson one of her diamond earrings.'

'If you ever mention that in a public space again, we're going to have to tussle. Can we go back to the beach now and at least pretend we're having a good time?'

It's strangely scary to have the full support of everyone I love. For the first time in my life I feel I am being backed up by my own personal battalion. My own army of misfits and weirdos.

I follow Matt back to the beach feeling as if I know the secret all these happy smiles are trying to hide from me. For once I am an insider, I get the joke. I'm not a sleepwalker any more.

Naomi

Ruby is in her room behind her closed door. She's been there for hours. I can hear her sobbing. Lily and Kumara comfort me on the sofa.

'She's young. When she gets over the shock, she'll see things completely differently,' says Kumara.

'I feel sure you've made the right decision,' Lily says quietly.

I seem to have reached some high cold place that's beyond right or wrong. Every cell in my body is telling me I've got no choice.

Over the next few days Lily and I start the necessary proceedings to have you adopted. Everyone keeps saying I'm being really brave and grown up. But if this is what being grown up means, I want to be a child for ever. I feel as if part of me has died. I can hardly get out of bed, let alone go to school and write essays on the Italian Renaissance.

It's Ruby who gets me out of my depression. She comes into my room one evening while Kumara's having a bath and says breathlessly, 'I just wanted to say that I was being a selfish little brat and thinking of myself and not about you at all, and I'm really really so sorry.'

She sits down on my bed and I hug her. 'I don't blame you for hating me. A lot of the time, I hate myself.'

Ruby's witchy green eyes are huge with pity. 'I don't hate you, Nomes. I want to help.'

'Ruby, you do, you do! Just by letting me live here with you all like this, taking up your space, monopolizing your sister and your mum.'

She scowls. 'Not just like that. That's nothing. I mean really help. If we're not going to have her for long, I want to make every day count.' There's a tear tracking down her cheek.

'Me too.' We're both snivelling. I lean across and wipe her face. 'You can help me with my stupid breathing exercises, for when I go into labour. You can help me knit her some little clothes if you like. That way when she goes to her new parents, they'll know we really loved her.'

'And *she'll* know,' Ruby whispers. 'I mean the baby.'

'Yes.'

We go into town and buy patterns, wool and needles, and in the evenings after school we sit knitting in front of the TV soaps.

If anything I'm worse than Ruby. The tiny fluffy sweater looks so simple in the pattern book, but I keep on dropping stitches. Lily shows me how to pick them up with a crochet hook but the delicate wool begins to split and fray from the constant unpicking.

'It'll look better once it's pressed,' Lily comforts me.

One morning we scrutinize my sorry handiwork by daylight and even Lily has to admit it's not looking too good. I'm in the depths of despair. Lily tells me briskly to get dressed and put my face on.

'I can't go to school,' I wail. 'I just can't.'

'Of course not, angel,' she says as if this is obvious. 'We're going into town so you can buy her something really lovely.'

Even though Lily has two overdue essays for college, she marches me off to catch the train and we go straight to John Lewis. After a great deal of agonizing I buy a pack of vests for newborns, three white babygros because I don't know which colour your new mother would prefer, and a tiny hooded bathrobe in fluffy white towelling. I'm taking a risk with the bathrobe. It has pink rosebuds round the hood and cuffs, and there's always that outside chance you'll turn out to be a boy. But somehow I don't think so.

When I've spent all my Café Esmeralda earnings, we go to the store cafeteria and Lily orders smoked salmon bagels and salad.

'Can you afford this?' I ask anxiously. 'You had to pay for my train ticket. And you were worried about the gas bill.'

'And I say fuck the gas bill,' she says. 'This is more important.'

I'm so touched I don't know what to say. 'I used to think you were like my second mum,' I say shyly.

She's carefully cutting her bagel into neat sections. I can see her wondering how to broach something. 'The fact is,' she says carefully, 'you have a fairly amazing mother of your own.'

'That's one way of putting it,' I mutter.

'Naomi, Allie can't be the easiest person in the world to have as your parent, but have you thought any more about patching things up with her?' Lily sees my face and quickly places her hand over mine. 'It's all right, angel. I'm not suggesting for one moment that you go back and live with her – just give her a call; hold out, you know, the hand of friendship, or whatever the cliché is.'

'I can't. If I get in touch with Mum now she'll find some way to make this be about *her*, and I haven't got the energy to fight her.'

'You'll have to face her some day.'

I shake my head. 'Not till this is all over. I've got to be strong to do what's right for me and my baby.'

My lip is trembling. To hide my feelings, I take all my baby purchases out of their carrier bag and pretend to examine them. They look totally inadequate and pathetic; the kind of tat you'd expect some sad un-married teenage mother to buy.

'She'll just throw them in the bin,' I say bleakly. 'I know I would.'

Lily sounds fierce. 'Well, I know I wouldn't.' She

strokes the tiny bathrobe tenderly. 'If I was adopting your baby, I'd be thrilled to have these little things. It'd be like a precious link between us. And when they were finally outgrown I'd wrap them up in tissue paper and keep them somewhere safe. I'd keep them until she was old enough to understand that she had two mothers, not just one.'

'Would you?' I whisper.

'I would, and so will she, Naomi, believe me.'

Carrie-Anne

That evening I wander down the beach, negotiating my way through the bodies of drunken revellers littering the sand. Like me, the sun has decided it is time to call it a day. To re-emerge to a new day full of unseen possibilities, beaming rays of comfort on those of us who are paying attention.

Naomi has called. She's called. After so many years of yearning, of hoping her presence in my life would act as some kind of miracle cure, healing all my pain and bewilderment, I'm shocked I feel so little. I'd expected her voice to be familiar. Soft, lyrical, lulling me back to her womb. But she was a stranger. Perhaps there would be answers: I'd see her and, like lightning striking an unsuspecting tree, I'd be split. Two halves: Naomi's face and my real father's face. I think back to a conversation Carl and I had a few months back.

I was in the library supposedly researching the evolution of man – or lack of it, as I eagerly pointed out. Carl was sitting opposite me, trying but failing to complete an art history essay that had been due weeks ago. He was slumped in his chair, looking as bored as I felt. 'I'm getting more attached to the idea that education should be optional.' He flicked an elastic band in my direction.

'If one of those hits me you are in big trouble, young man.' I rested my head on the table, examining close up the graffiti that had been etched into the tabletop. 'I'm going to find my mum.'

'When did you lose her? She seemed pretty visible last night.'

'I mean my biological mum.' I sat up and gave Carl what my dad refers to as 'the evil eye', irritated by his flippancy.

'I know what you meant. But you've been going on about it for so long, I didn't know you were serious.'

'I'm deadly serious. I want to know where I come from, where I fit in, in this world.'

He shook his head. 'No parent can do that. Your parents can fill you in on all that family history crap, but they can't give you a place in the world. I unfortunately am acquainted with both of my loving parents, and I'm still clueless.' He flicked another elastic band at me.

'You don't know how it feels not knowing where you come from! How can I move forward without knowing?' I was trying not to cry. I wanted Carl to say the right thing, be understanding, and he just wasn't playing.

'Like the rest of us, by putting one foot in front of the other. Like they say, the destination isn't important; how you get there is the crucial part.'

'Well, whatever, I wouldn't expect *you* to understand – in fact any of you.'

But Carl had been right. I'd been searching for easy answers. I'd been screaming at the top of my lungs for someone to come and save me, rescue me from myself. The call hadn't been answered. It never would be: there were no lifeguards who could retrieve me from my ocean of confusion. I was going to have to battle the currents of chaos and uncertainty by myself to reach the safety of solid and dry land. Like Carl said, I just had to keep moving forward. Carrie-Anne Harris, destination unknown.

Naomi

One morning I get up and I can't get my shoes on.

'Help!' I wail. 'Even my feet are getting fat.'

Lily is peering short-sightedly into Kumara's mirror, putting in some hoop earrings. 'It's water retention,' she says. 'Before Kumara was born, my hands swelled up so badly, I couldn't get my wedding ring off.'

'Coo-er, a wedding ring,' Ruby calls as she pads past on her way to the bathroom. 'Those were the days.'

Lily turns to Kumara. 'I don't know,' she says. 'Maybe we shouldn't go. What do you think?'

'I think we shouldn't go too,' says Kumara. She looks extraordinarily beautiful in the black shirt dress Lily bought her for today's audition and which she insisted on wearing with her old Doc Martens.

'You're just chicken,' I tell her.

'I am not chicken, Nomes,' she says. 'I just don't want

to go swanning off to London for the day and end up missing the main event.'

'There isn't going to be an event. Not yet. I've got two weeks to go according to the doctor.'

'And you aren't still having any of those whatever they're called – Hixton Bracks thingies?' Kumara asks.

'Braxton Hicks contractions,' I say. 'Not for ages.'

Kumara and Lily make up their minds to go to London after all. They get all the way to the front door, then come back again and hover anxiously. 'Angel, are you sure you really feel OK?' says Lily.

'May I just point out that I'm no longer five years old,' says Ruby irritably. 'I'm every bit as capable of phoning for an ambulance as either of you two.'

'Exactly,' I tell them. 'Anyway, first babies are always late and they take absolutely hours and hours to come out, everyone knows that.'

'Thank God for that,' says Ruby as her mum and sister finally go off to catch the train. 'Now we can watch rubbish on TV in peace.'

'I'll watch rubbish with you later,' I say. 'I've got an

essay to write on some artist called Jackson Pollock.'

'Is he that guy who used to spatter paint on his canvasses?'

'He cycled across them too. I think I read somewhere that he actually painted one canvas using his penis.'

Ruby covers her ears. 'Ugh, that is so gross! He sounds like a total pervert.'

'He was a total genius,' I correct her.

She gives me a wicked grin. 'He was probably a genius with a very *very* sore penis.'

I go and curl up on my bed with a notepad and try to think where to start. There's a strange squeezing sensation in my lower abdomen, which makes it hard to get comfortable. I decide I'm having one of my practice contractions after all, so I get up again and walk about, taking deep breaths, waiting for it to pass. But the squeezing just gets more intense.

I find myself hanging onto the chest of drawers, gasping with effort.

Suddenly Ruby's in the doorway, looking white. 'Nomes?' she says. 'What's happening?'

I just wave at her apologetically, then the contraction

225

eases off and I say, 'Sorry, this sort of takes all your concentration.'

'Should I phone for an ambulance?'

'I think maybe you should.'

Ruby dashes off, whimpering, 'Oh my God, oh my God.' She's in such a panic she forgets to tell the ambulance service where we live and has to call them back.

We sit on the sofa clutching each other's hands, waiting for the ambulance. Each time I get another contraction she does my breathing exercises with me. They usually make us roll around the floor in hysterics but we're too scared to find them funny now.

'Do you want me to come with you?' Ruby offers bravely. 'I'm all right with blood. It's vomit I can't do. Does having a baby make you vomit?'

'Don't worry, Ruby, I don't think they'd let you anyway.'

She bursts into tears. 'But you'll be all alone. And I want to see her.'

'I'll be OK, honestly,' I say, though my teeth are chattering with fear. 'You can come and see her just as soon as she's born.'

The ambulance pulls up outside and Ruby races to let them in. 'Have her waters broken?' I hear one of the men ask.

She sounds appalled. 'What's that?'

'No,' I call. 'Not yet.'

The paramedics come into the living room.

'Morning, young lady,' says the big fatherly one. 'Got your bag all packed?'

'It's by the door,' says Ruby.

'How far apart are the contractions?' asks his mate.

'I'm h-having one now,' I gasp.

They wait patiently until it passes.

'Can you walk to the ambulance?'

I nod. 'I think so.'

I totter cautiously down the path with the two paramedics for support. Curtains twitch all along the road but I'm past caring.

I turn round and see Ruby looking desperate on the step.

'I'll call you, I promise!' I yell.

The men help me into the back of the ambulance and we speed off, with the siren wailing.

The paramedic tucks a soft red blanket around me. He's talking to me in a soothing voice, as if I'm some small scared animal, telling me not to worry, they'll have me at the hospital in a couple of ticks, but I'm gazing completely hypnotized at the blanket, because I've just remembered the dream I had last night.

In my dream I'd already given birth to you. I wasn't expecting you to come so soon and I was ransacking cupboards and drawers in a panic to find something suitable to keep you warm.

In desperation I tipped my hospital bag upside down and out fell the most exquisite cot quilt. It had been hand-stitched with a complicated star pattern in the kind of magical colours you only see in dreams, deep ocean-blues and glowing crimsons.

I gazed at it, wondering where this miraculous thing had come from, and it gradually dawned on me that I had made it myself, out of scraps cut from our old Wonder Girl costumes.

I wrapped the starry quilt gently around you and you suddenly opened your eyes and looked at me.

And as I held you close, I was filled with this amazing

sense of peace, because I had something good enough to give you at last.

jan mark
Something
in the Air

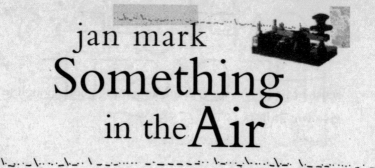

Ever since a visit to the dentist, Peggy has been hearing the
oddest noises reverberating in her head. It's not clanging
water pipes, or creaking floorboards from outside, or music,
or humming in her own mind. In fact what it really sounds
like is Morse code – a rapid staccato of dots and dashes of
the sort used by radio operators in the Great War just a few
years before. But why would anyone be transmitting Morse
code that fast – through Peggy's head?

Who can Peggy confide in? The only possibility is her
young aunt, Stella – a true friend and trusted confidante.
But instead of the reassuring response Peggy expects from
her aunt, Stella has an uncharacteristically disturbing
explanation for the strange sounds.

Could the noise in Peggy's head really be a message from
the past, from a world beyond the grave?

*A finely wrought picture of a girl's life in 1920's England from
Jan Mark, twice winner of the Carnegie Medal.*

DEFINITIONS
0–099–43234–X

I CAPTURE
THE CASTLE
DODIE SMITH

This wonderful novel tells the story of seventeen-year-old Cassandra and her extraordinary family, who live in not-so-genteel poverty in a ramshackle old English castle.

Cassandra's eccentric father is a writer whose first book took the literary world by storm but he has since failed to write a single word and now spends most of his time reading detective novels from the village library. Cassandra's elder sister, Rose - exquisitely beautiful, vain and bored - despairs of her family's circumstances and determines to marry their affluent American landlord, Simon, despite the fact she does not love him. She is in turns helped and hindered in this by their bohemian step-mother Topaz, an artist's model and nudist who likes to commune with nature. Finally there is Stephen, dazzlingly handsome and hopelessly in love with Cassandra.

Amidst the maelstrom Cassandra strives to hone her writing skills. She fills three notebooks with sharply funny yet poignant entries, which candidly chronicle the great changes that take place within the castle's walls, and her own first descent into love. By the time she pens her final entry, she has captured the heart of the reader in one of literature's most enchanting entertainments.

DEFINITIONS
0 09 984500 8

Remembrance

THERESA BRESLIN

Summer 1915, and the sound of the guns at the Western Front can be heard across the Channel in England. Throughout Britain, local regiments are recruiting for Kitchener's Army. And in the village of Stratharden, the Great War has already begun to irrevocably alter the course of five young lives…

'It's up to us now. I can't wait to get to the Front and be with my friends. I hope it's not all over before I get there.'
JOHN MALCOLM

'I'm not trying to look respectable, I'm trying to be useful. I intend to volunteer for nursing in France.'
CHARLOTTE

'I am strangely unafraid of death . . . what frightens me more is the death of spirit, that I have so quickly become accustomed to the sights and sounds of war . . .'
FRANCIS

'There are opportunities for women now, and I mean to take them. I am set to determine my own course in life.'
MAGGIE

'I may be too young, but I am going to enlist. And I will get away with it.'
ALEX

An epic novel from the award-winning author Theresa Breslin.

Read it - and remember…

CORGI BOOKS
0 552 54738 7

LINDA NEWBERY

THE
SHELL
HOUSE

When Greg stumbles across the beautiful ruins of Graveney
Hall, he becomes intrigued by the story behind its
destruction. He and his friend Faith are drawn into a quest
to discover the fate of Graveney's last heir, Edmund, a
young soldier who disappeared in mysterious circumstances
during the First World War.

But Greg's investigations force him to question his own
views on love and faith, and reveal more about himself
than he would ever have imagined.

*A beautiful portrayal of love, sexuality and
spirituality over two generations.*

'Intelligent and perceptive'
GUARDIAN
'Newbery writes wonderfully'
FINANCIAL TIMES
'This is a novel to read, think about, and then read again'
INDEPENDENT

SHORTLISTED FOR THE GUARDIAN CHILDREN'S FICTION PRIZE
SHORTLISTED FOR THE CARNEGIE MEDAL

DEFINITIONS
0 099 45593 5

C⊕RBENIC

CATHERINE FISHER

Cal has struggled to cope with his mother's drinking and psychotic episodes since he was six; so when he finally leaves home to live with his uncle he is ruthless about breaking with the past, despite his mother's despair. But getting off the train at the wrong station, Cal finds himself at the mysterious castle of the Fisher King; and the night he spends there plunges him into a wasteland of desolation and adventure as he begins his predetermined quest back to all he has betrayed.

In this intriguing reworking of the Grail Legend, the award-winning author Catherine Fisher has created a gripping novel that moves between myth and a contemporary journey of self-knowledge until one becomes indistinguishable from the other.

'An elaborate and intricate reworking of the Grail Legend...an absorbing story' *BOOKSELLER*

Shortlisted for the Tir Na nOg Prize

DEFINITIONS
0 09 943848 8